JEFFREY STANDISH
d.1194
(Escape from France)

SIR HENRY CAREY Bart.
d.1835

CAPTAIN CHRISTOPHER CAREY
d.1812
(Captain of Foot)

American Descendants

OLIVER CAREY
d.1798

LIEUTENANT-COLONEL
RICHARD CAREY 8th Earl
d.1859
(Escape from France & Captain of Foot)

SIR ROBERT CAREY
d.1870
(Nicholas Carey)

ADMIRAL
SIR PETER CAREY
Bart
d.1850 (Captain of Foot)

COLONEL NICHOLAS CAREY
d.1910
(Nicholas Carey & Ensign Carey)

ANDREW CAREY
d.1905
(Nicholas Carey)

CAPTAIN (later Admiral)
SIR JOHN CAREY
Bart. RN
d.1885
(Nicholas Carey & Ensign Carey)

WILLIAM CAREY
d.1857
(Ensign Carey)

GENERAL SIR PETER
Bart
d.1940 (Tank Comd.)

GENERAL SIR JOHN
Bart.
(Tank Commander)

JAMES CAREY 9th Earl
d.1868
(Nicholas Carey)

BERNARD CAREY 10th Earl
d.1902
(Nicholas Carey)

CAPTAIN SIR EDWARD CAREY
Bart. RN
d.1911 (Ensign Carey)

MARY CAREY   m.
d.1937

CHARLES CAREY 11th Earl
d.1936

ESCAPE FROM FRANCE

Ronald Welch's series of twelve Carey novels, published between 1954 and 1976, follows the fortunes of a Welsh landowning family from their involvement in the Crusades to service in the First World War. Though the books were not written chronologically, put together they join up the dots of English history. A Carey plays a part in the Battle of Crécy and another helps foil a plot to assassinate Queen Elizabeth. The Battle of Blenheim, Wolfe's victory at Quebec, the French Revolution, the Peninsular War, the Crimea, the Indian Mutiny – in each volume a Carey is in the thick of it.

Their creator, Ronald Oliver Felton (1909–82), was a history teacher who served as a Tank Corps officer in the Second World War and took the pen-name Welch from that of his wartime regiment. In 1947 he became Headmaster of Okehampton Grammar School in Devon. Pupils describe him as an inspiring teacher who looked, sounded and dressed like a typical upper-class Englishman – though in fact it was Wales, the land of his fathers, that was his spiritual home. The Careys too have a much-loved Welsh estate, Llanstephan, and Wales features strongly in the books.

The far-flung places Welch wrote about he recreated entirely from meticulous research. Oxford University Press, who first published his books, considered him so knowledgeable that he was often called on to check the work of other authors for accuracy. His first historical novel for children, *The Gauntlet*, was published in 1951. The first in the Carey series, *Knight Crusader*, which won the Carnegie Medal for the most outstanding children's book of the year, was published in 1954. The Carey books have unaccountably been out of print for many years. Now, for the first time, Slightly Foxed is reissuing them in their entirety, together with their original illustrations. For a complete list see overleaf.

Escape from France

RONALD WELCH

Illustrated by
William Stobbs

First published by Oxford University Press in 1960
First published by Slightly Foxed in 2015
in a limited edition of 2,000 copies
of which this is copy No.

509

Cover illustration by Daniel Macklin
© Ronald Welch 1960
Illustrations © William Stobbs 1960

Slightly Foxed Ltd
53 Hoxton Square
London N1 6PB

A CIP catalogue record for this book is available from the British Library.

ISBN 978-1-906562-72-4

Printed by Smith Settle, Yeadon, West Yorkshire

Contents

I

Cambridge

Richard Carey leant back against the panelled wall and yawned. The sun that streamed through the long windows made him drowsy, and the deep, booming voice of Dr Emmanuel Walker expounding the development of the Greek city states was a soothing sound.

Richard yawned again and tried to fight the pleasant sense of sleepiness that was drifting over him. Through half-closed eyes he inspected the huge portrait of King Henry the Eighth that hung over the dais and above the white head of Dr Walker, a stout and dignified figure in black coat and breeches, one plump hand fluttering gracefully in the air to illustrate some point in his lecture.

Richard's sleepy glance moved down the hall, over the dark, polished tables and the bent heads of undergraduates, and came to rest on his cousin, Jeffery Standish. Richard half smiled, for Jeffery was scribbling busily, one hand ruffling his fair hair, his forehead crinkled in thought. Richard's smile broadened; he would bet quite a large sum that Jeffery was not making a careful note of the politics of Pericles; he was probably trying to work out the runners for the races at Newmarket that afternoon.

Richard wriggled himself into a more comfortable position and turned his head to watch Bellamy, sitting at the end of the table. Bellamy was at Richard's college, a small, thin young man with a pallid, bony face, and a high forehead over which fell his black, untidy hair. He was listening intently to the lecture, one hand moving steadily across the page of his notebook in neat lines of precise writing.

Richard shifted again, and this time he closed his eyes. Cambridge, he decided, was becoming an extremely boring place.

A hand shook his shoulder. 'Wake up, Richard! Old Walker's just finished.'

Richard sat up hurriedly and closed his notebook. 'Hello, Jeffery,' he said. 'I must have gone to sleep.'

'You're been snoring for the last half-hour. Come and have a drink in my rooms before we go.'

Richard nodded and pushed his way unceremoniously through the men standing outside the buttery hatches, and out on to the steps and the broad expanse of Trinity Great Court. He was hailed there by a young man in a pea-green coat, very tight breeches and Hessian boots.

'Hello, Carey. Going to Newmarket?'

'Yes, Murray. I'm taking Standish,' Richard said curtly, and eyeing Sir John Murray without much enthusiasm.

'I say, Carey,' Murray said, mouthing and broadening his vowels in the fashionable London accent of the day, 'my stableman tells me that Percival is a good outside bet for the Langley Stakes. Know anything about him, eh?'

'Ask Standish, he's the expert,' Richard said, and he walked on, until he stopped irritably as he felt a hesitant hand touch the sleeve of his coat. He sighed and looked down into the white face of Mr Bellamy.

'I beg your pardon, Mr Carey,' and Bellamy smiled nervously, his brown eyes as pleading as those of any spaniel. 'But I noticed that you had fallen asleep during the lecture. Dr Walker was particularly interesting about the development of the Athenian constitution. Particularly interesting.'

Richard nodded and put on his tall beaver hat, ready to move on. But Bellamy, despite his nervousness, was a persistent young man, and he was accustomed to snubs.

'I took very full notes, Mr Carey. Very full,' he said. 'If they would be of any assistance to you, I would be honoured if you would borrow them. Honoured.'

Richard opened his mouth to deliver one of those biting snubs for which he was notorious in Cambridge. But Bellamy hurried on.

'Or perhaps I can leave them in your rooms, Mr Carey. Yes, in your rooms.' There was a loud crack, and Richard glanced down. Bellamy was tugging at the big joints of his fingers, and with each twitch there came another crack.

Richard tried again. 'If you will excuse me, Bellamy, but I . . .'

'Going to Newmarket, I expect, Mr Carey? In your new curricle? A beautiful vehicle! Beautiful!' Another series of cracks, and Bellamy beamed up nervously.

Richard wondered what irritated him most, the little man's nervous persistence, his infuriating habit of repetition at the end of each sentence, or those nauseating cracks from his finger-joints. Perhaps a swift retreat was the best solution, so he bowed stiffly, and turned away.

'I say, Carey,' came Murray's high-pitched drawl, 'who's that odd-looking fellow? Not a friend of yours, surely?' He made no attempt to lower his voice, even though the unfortunate Bellamy was still standing a few feet away.

'His name is Bellamy,' Richard said furiously, still walking quickly. 'His father is an attorney and handles all our family affairs.'

He turned abruptly, dived through a doorway and clattered up the bare wooden stairs that led to Jeffery's rooms. Five minutes with Bellamy were tedious enough, but a conversation with a brainless fool like Sir John

Murray was more than he could stomach in his present mood.

There were several other men in Jeffery's room, drinking and talking, but Richard ignored their nods and greetings with crashing rudeness, picked up a filled glass and a newspaper, and crossed to the windows overlooking the court.

The paper would be a week old, if he knew anything of Jeffery, and he looked at the date before he turned to the inside pages: 21 June 1791. Two days old, he thought, as he ran his eye down the paragraphs dealing with foreign affairs.

The news from Paris was brief and startling. King Louis, the Queen and all the Royal family had escaped from Paris and were believed to be making for the German frontier. Already a petition had been submitted to the Assembly for the proclamation of a Republic.

Richard whistled softly. He might sleep through lectures on the constitution of Athens, though he had read far more widely on that subject than many of his friends suspected, but he followed the politics of Europe with an intelligent and well-informed interest.

Well, this would put the cat among the pigeons, he thought. If Louis got clean away, then the extremists in the Assembly would have a free hand, and a wonderful chance to seize power for themselves. And the King, safely over the frontier, would bombard the Powers for help to recover his throne. Austria, for one, would help, and perhaps Prussia too. That would mean war, and England would find it difficult to remain aloof.

Richard pulled out his fob-watch. Time to leave for Newmarket. He wished he could hear his father's opinion on the news, for Lord Aubigny, with a post in the Government, could have given him a shrewd forecast of what might happen in the next few months.

Anyway, Paris would be in an uproar, Richard thought, as he looked down at the peaceful scene in the court below, the strolling undergraduates, the group of dons chatting by the Porter's lodge, and the general atmosphere of leisure and tranquillity. Richard tried to remember Paris as he had last seen it, ten years ago as a boy, visiting his French relations.

They would be in Normandy probably, unless the Marquis de Vernaye had already emigrated with many of his friends. Richard finished his glass of wine. He was never quite clear about his exact relationship with the Assailly family, for there had been no marriages between them and the Careys for several generations. But the connection was scrupulously maintained, and Richard had a faint suspicion that he was intended by both sides to draw the relationship closer; there had been mutters of cousin Louise, but Richard could barely remember what she looked like, beyond a vague recollection of a dark-haired child who never opened her mouth.

He pushed his watch back in the tight little pocket in his breeches, and called out peremptorily, 'Come on, Jeffery; time we went!'

He did not wait for any answer but strode through the door. Jeffery shrugged his shoulders, grimaced apologetically to his guests and hurried after his cousin. The other men grinned; they were accustomed to Richard's manners, which alternated abruptly between downright rudeness and arrogance, and sudden spasms of charm and friendliness.

Richard's new curricle, the object of Bellamy's respectful comment, was waiting outside the gates of Trinity. Two undergraduates were admiring it, and Richard ignored them. He did not know them, but they knew him by sight, and he was fully aware of that fact.

The curricle was indeed a beautiful vehicle, the work of a London coachbuilder, with its two wheels, high body and highly polished woodwork, over which Richard ran his eye. A curricle was no vehicle for a beginner to drive, for with its height and speed it would overturn only too easily.

Richard drew on a pair of thin gloves, and climbed up beside Jeffery. 'Let 'em go, Tom,' he said curtly to his groom.

The horses leapt forward, and the curricle swayed and jolted over the cobbles; then they were clip-clopping down Trinity Street, while Richard picked his way through the carts and wagons. His irritation had vanished, and he whistled soundlessly as he inserted the curricle between a coach and a phaeton standing by the pavement, slid through the gap with a few inches to spare, and smiled at the startled face of the coachman.

There was little for him to do once they had left Cambridge behind and were rolling smoothly down the straight road to Newmarket. He looked up at the blue sky and the snowy white clouds, and then over the flat countryside around them. He missed the mountains of his native Wales, for he had an eye for beautiful scenery, though he would never have admitted the fact to any of his Cambridge acquaintances. But then there was a great deal that Cambridge did not know about Richard.

Jeffery heard the soft whistling and smiled. He knew his cousin better than most people, and was fond of him too. A pity, he was thinking, that Richard did not show the pleasanter side of his character more often; to his acquaintances – and that was all they were, rather than friends – Richard was arrogant, rude and intolerant of stupidity. But he was respected and men deferred to him; after all, he was Lord Aubigny's heir, a dangerous man with his hands and weapons, and his searing snubs and biting tongue were feared.

Richard was suddenly conscious that his cousin was silent, a rare state of affairs, for Jeffery was usually extremely talkative. Richard glanced to his side, and his forehead crinkled slightly, for Jeffery's face was an easy one to read.

'What's the trouble, Jeffery?'

Jeffery hesitated; his hands were clenched, the fingers working uneasily. 'I've backed Lyonesse for the Langley Stakes,' he said.

'What of it?' Richard said casually. 'How much?'

'Five hundred,' Jeffery said defiantly.

The horses threw up their heads as Richard's hand tightened on the reins. He grunted and swung out to pass a well-loaded coach.

'Where in the devil's name did you get five hundred pounds from?' he demanded.

'I sold out from the Funds.'

Richard nodded. At the age of twenty-one Jeffery had been given control of his share; his father had done so deliberately on the theory that the sooner Jeffery learnt how to handle money the better.

'But why so much, Jeffery?'

'I was given odds of ten to one.'

Richard was startled. 'You stand to win five thousand!' he said. 'You must be pretty desperate, Jeffery.'

'Who said I was desperate?' Jeffery said. 'Wouldn't you pick up five thousand if you had the chance?'

'If I wanted it badly enough. I think you do. Don't you?'

He watched his cousin's hands. Hands could reveal a great deal, he thought.

'Yes, I've *got* to win this afternoon, Richard.'

Richard saw a narrow lane just ahead on the right, and he swung the curricle across the road and pulled up with a jerk beneath a huge tree.

'I think it's time you told me what sort of mess you've landed yourself in,' he said.

Jeffery laughed shrilly. 'If Lyonesse loses I'm finished,' he said.

Richard snorted. 'Don't be a fool,' he said sharply. 'What do you mean, finished? What have you been up to, Jeffery?'

The coach they had just passed rattled by; the outside passengers were singing cheerfully at the prospect of a good day's racing at Newmarket. Jeffery turned to watch them enviously, and stuffed his shaking hands deep into the pockets of his fawn breeches.

'It started eighteen months ago,' he said. 'In London. I met a Captain Walton at Father's club. D'you know him, Richard?'

'Yes, I do. He's a shark.'

Jeffery nodded gloomily. 'He's a pretty hungry one. He took me to a place called Naylor's. I suppose you've heard of it?'

'I have. You fool! Go on!'

'Well, I won that night,' Jeffery said indignantly.

'Of course you did! They always let the pigeon win at first. And then you lost regularly.'

'Not every night. They were pretty clever.'

'Oh, yes, they're clever,' Richard said angrily. 'It's their profession, after all, and you need some wits if you have to live by them. But you were under twenty-one then, Jeffery. Where did you find the money? Money-lenders?'

'Yes. Walton introduced me to one. Very accommodating he was, too,' Jeffery said ruefully. 'I explained that I wasn't of age but that I would come into something in a year's time. They seemed to know that.'

Richard sighed. He was the same age as his cousin, but Jeffery's pitiful little tale made him feel many years older.

'How do you think money-lenders live?' he asked. 'Well, you borrowed, and then you began to sell when you were of age. Didn't you clear yourself?'

'No, Walton egged me on, and last summer, when you were down at Llanstephan, I lost night after night. I'm not a very good gambler, you know, Richard.'

'You aren't,' Richard said bluntly. 'Have you got anything left?'

'Not a penny.'

Richard turned to his cousin. 'But why didn't you tell me?' he asked.

'You're not the easiest of people to confide in, Richard, are you?' Jeffery said quietly.

Richard opened his mouth to protest. Then he paused, and began to turn the curricle. 'No, I suppose I'm not,' he said. For a moment he had seen himself as he appeared to others, and the picture was not a pleasant one.

'Well, I want some food before the races start,' he said. 'Uncle Robert doesn't know anything of this, of course?'

'No. Father doesn't know.'

'Well, I can't help you,' Richard said. 'I've no capital of my own yet, but I can let you have something from my allowance.'

'That won't go far,' Jeffery said. 'Anyway, Lyonesse will win.'

'He'll have to,' Richard said grimly. 'Here's Newmarket, at last.'

They drove slowly down the long main street of the little town, crowded already with carriages and horses, and Richard manoeuvred his curricle into the yard of the White Hart, three-quarters filled with chaises, curricles, phaetons and every conceivable variety of carriage.

Richard hailed an ostler, who recognized him as a frequent visitor.

'Take my horses, Will.'

'In a minute, Mr Carey.'

'Now,' Richard said, 'or it's the last tip you get from me.'

'But these are Lord Dawnay's horses I'm looking after, Mr Carey!'

'I don't care if they belong to the Sultan of Turkey,' Richard said. He jumped down, thrust the reins into the ostler's hands and marched into the inn. The ostler scratched his head, but as Jeffery looked back from the door he saw the man backing Richard's curricle into a vacant place.

A clatter of dishes and a smell of cooking greeted them inside the inn, and the landlord hurried up as he saw Richard.

'Good morning, Mr Carey. The coffee-room is full at the moment. A glass of wine while you wait?'

Richard pulled out his watch. 'I sent my man over last week to reserve me a table at one o'clock,' he said. 'It's one now, and there's an empty table by the door. Mr Standish and I will take that, Plowden.'

Plowden rubbed his hands together uneasily. 'But I have just given that table to two other gentlemen, Mr Carey.'

'Then they'll have to wait, won't they?' Richard said, pulling back one of the chairs. 'Two tankards of beer, please, Plowden, and some of that beef.'

A hand fell on Richard's shoulder and twisted him round.

'And who the devil do you think you are?' a voice demanded. 'That's my table, and Major Morlock of the 52nd doesn't take a back seat to a couple of young sprigs from Cambridge.'

Richard caught the hand on his shoulder and pulled it down slowly and without any apparent effort. But the other winced and rubbed his wrist. He was a florid-faced man, very well dressed – perhaps a trifle too well dressed to Richard's critical eye, who wondered if this fellow had ever really seen the inside of the officers' mess of the 52nd. Morlock hesitated for a moment as he inspected Richard with the practised skill of a man who makes his living by summing up young men of Richard's type. He noticed the cut of the coat and breeches, the powerful shoulders, the chilly grey eyes that were watching him, and the general attitude of arrogance and self-confidence. But he had been drinking, and he was in no mood for caution.

'Look here . . .' he began, when another man caught his elbow and pulled him away hastily.

'There's an empty place over there, Morlock,' he said. 'Come and have a drink while the waiter lays the table.' As they went out of the room, Jeffery caught the end of their conversation. 'Don't you know young Carey, Morlock? Aubigny's son. He's no pigeon. Tanner had an argument with him last month and finished with a broken nose. Damn your eyes and take that, is . . .'

Jeffery smiled ruefully as he watched Richard eating. His cousin took all this so much for granted. One day he would find himself in trouble, and that, Jeffery thought, might be no bad thing.

'Come on, eat up,' Richard said briskly. 'Do you good!'

'I feel as sick as a dog,' Jeffery confessed.

'You'll feel worse if Lyonesse loses.' Richard put down his tankard. 'What will you do?'

'Run for it.'

'Don't be a fool. Tell Uncle Robert.'

'Would you?' Jeffery asked.

Richard grunted. Jeffery was probably right. Sir Robert Standish was a kindly and affectionate father, but he would be furious when he heard how Jeffery had squandered his money. And he was a rigid Churchman with a horror of gambling; his icy rage could be frightening, and Richard could guess the effect on Jeffery, with his obstinacy and quick temper. He was quite capable of running for it, and goodness knows where he might finish.

They reached the Heath with an hour to spare before the start of the Langley Stakes, and Richard found a man to look after his horses, brushed the dust from his boots, adjusted his cravat and tried not to feel uneasy. Jeffery's strained face, the nervous clenching and unclenching of his hands were having their effect on his cousin, too.

'Let's have a look at Lyonesse,' Jeffery said, and he pushed his way through the crowd towards the enclosure.

'Looks fit enough, doesn't he?' Jeffery asked.

Richard inspected the big grey and nodded, his spirits rising slightly. Perhaps Jeffery had picked a winner, after all.

'Backing him, Carey?' a voice asked.

Richard turned and bowed respectfully as he saw Lord Surridge, a friend of his father and a noted and successful breeder of bloodstock.

'What do you think of him, sir?' he asked, and Jeffery, despite his anxiety, smiled broadly at the note in his cousin's voice. For Richard did possess one virtue: he was invariably polite to his elders.

The old gentleman rubbed his nose reflectively. 'Well bred,' he said slowly. 'In beautiful condition. But will he stay the distance, eh?' and he nodded to Richard and strolled away.

'He'll stay all right,' Jeffery said, but there was a tinge of doubt in his voice.

'Sure to,' Richard said encouragingly, though he had never felt less certain of anything. Lord Surridge was too much of an expert on horses for his liking.

They found a place in the stand from where they could see the finish, and Jeffery shifted restlessly from one foot to the other as the horses went down to the start.

'The odds have shortened,' he said. 'Lyonesse is the favourite. They usually know, Richard.'

'They certainly do,' Richard said heartily, wondering how often a heavily backed favourite had failed to win. Both races that afternoon had been won by long-priced horses.

'They're off!' Jeffery said.

'No,' Richard murmured, and there was another wait in the distance as the horses circled and gradually formed up into a line.

'Doesn't that starter know his business?' Jeffery said. 'There's Lyonesse on the left. Lucky he's a grey. We can see him all the way.'

A roar went up from the crowd, and the line of horses swept forward.

'Can't see him,' Jeffery muttered. 'Boxed in, isn't he?'

'I don't know,' Richard said. 'And don't twist my arm off, Jeffery.'

The horses were bunched into one small group now as they came up the long straight, still so far away that they seemed to be trotting, so slowly did they approach.

'There he is,' Jeffery whispered into Richard's ear. 'Lying third.'

The pace seemed to quicken as the horses neared the stands, and the crowd began to bellow.

'Three furlongs to go,' Jeffery said, and his voice rose to a shrill scream as the grey shot to the front, and began to draw away. Richard was pushed aside, and only by standing on tiptoe could he see the race, while Jeffery jumped and waved his hat, his mouth wide open, his face red with excitement and the effort of shouting his horse home.

The roar of the crowd suddenly died down, and a single stentorian voice could be heard, yelling, 'Percival wins! Percival wins!'

Richard felt his mouth go dry, and he was quite unaware of Jeffery's hand clutching his wrist as a black horse crept past Lyonesse, gaining at every stride, until the grey disappeared in the group of horses behind.

2

Sir Robert Standish

Richard cleared his throat. 'Well, he wasn't a stayer, after all,' he said.

Jeffery shook his head. The blood had drained from his face, and he was staring across the Heath, his whole body shaking. Shock, Richard thought, and he pushed his cousin through the crowd towards the curricle. From a small locker beneath the seat he produced a silver flask.

'Drink that,' he said.

Jeffery gulped down the brandy, coughed and drew a deep breath. 'Thanks, Richard. Feeling better now,' he said.

'Might as well drive back before the crowd leaves,' Richard suggested.

Jeffery nodded. 'The sooner the better,' he said, and he climbed up into the high seat.

'Mr Carey, Mr Carey!'

Richard turned sharply. He knew that voice, and with dismay he saw Bellamy running towards them.

'What's the matter?' Richard demanded impatiently. A conversation with Bellamy now would be intolerable.

'Can you help us, Mr Carey? A bookmaker won't pay us. We backed Percival. I heard Sir John Murray say he would win, and he did.'

He looked appealingly up at Richard's stormy face, and in his agitation he had not repeated himself once, but he was tugging nervously at his fingers, and Richard heard the familiar crack of the joints. It needed only that to complete his growing fury. Jeffery, the presumed expert on race-horses for whom a win had been almost a matter of life or death, had lost. And this stupid clod, who probably never saw a horse except from the outside seat of a stage-coach, had won. The world was indeed a bitterly unjust place, Richard thought, as he glared down into Bellamy's pleading face.

'Let's go and see this fellow,' Jeffery said briskly, jumping down to the ground. He seemed glad of the chance to forget his own troubles.

Richard hesitated. Then the prospect of action, the possibility of venting his fury on someone else, made him nod his head. He stalked after Bellamy's shambling figure like an avenging angel, and pushed his way roughly into the centre of a shouting group of undergraduates. They fell back as they recognized him, and several voices all appealed to him at once. Bellamy turned towards the bookmaker.

'Here's the Honourable Mr Carey,' he said impressively.

The bookmaker was a plump and flashily dressed man with a tight blue coat and white breeches. He scowled at Richard.

'And what do you want, my young sprig of fashion?' he asked.

Richard ignored him. 'How much does he owe you?' he asked Bellamy.

A chorus of shouts went up. 'Did he give you tickets?' Richard asked, and he nodded as he saw the flourished pieces of paper.

'Pay up,' he said curtly to the bookmaker, 'or I'll have you run off the Heath.'

The bookmaker smirked. 'I can't, my lad, so that's that.'

'Oh, yes, he can, Mr Carey,' Bellamy said quickly. 'He took a lot of money on the favourite. That bag of his is stuffed with money. Stuffed!' he added, to the accompaniment of a loud crack from his fingers.

A burly figure pushed his way in front of the bookmaker, a bandy-legged man in a rusty brown coat, with wide shoulders, a bent nose and two flattened ears. Ex-prize fighter run to seed, Richard thought instinctively. All these bookies had some form of protection. But even run-down ex-pugs probably retained a punch like the kick of a horse, and Richard felt a delightful thrill run through him.

'Now, orf with yer,' the pugilist said. 'You 'eard. Mr Sanders can't pay up. Me 'eart bleeds for yer, but that's the luck of the game.'

'Bob Towler, Mr Carey,' one of the undergraduates muttered in Richard's ear. 'Went six rounds with Cribb.'

Richard nodded. He had no intention of going more than one round with this fellow. He prodded Towler in the stomach with his cane.

'Out of the way,' he said contemptuously.

The effect was exactly what he had expected and wanted. Towler growled angrily and let fly with his right in a swinging punch. But Richard had been watching him; the faintest flicker in Towler's eyes was enough. The clenched fist whistled over his head, and with a smack his own right went home on the pugilist's heavy jowl.

He was off balance, and surprised; a counter-punch from this young exquisite was the last thing he had expected, and he toppled backwards and went sprawling on the grass.

But out of condition as he was, he had been trained to take punches like this, and he was up almost immediately. But he had lost his temper, and with it his fighter's judgement. He swung wildly at Richard, took a sickening blow in his stomach, gasped and threw back his head, and another right caught him full on the point of his jaw. As he went down for the second time, the back of his head cracked against the wheel of a coach, and he rolled over on the turf, arms outflung, motionless.

'Now pay up, Sanders, if that's your name,' Richard said.

The bookmaker had tried to edge away, but he was surrounded by a

ring of threatening faces. He cursed, but he dived into his thick bag and began to hand out notes. Richard smiled as he heard the crack of finger-joints by his side.

'I am very grateful, Mr Carey,' Bellamy said. 'Very grateful.'

'See that he pays in full,' Richard said. 'I don't think he'll try and welch you again, though.'

He walked back briskly with Jeffery to the curricle, feeling a good deal happier than he had been for some time. Even Jeffery forgot his troubles and chatted about Towler's record in the prize ring while Richard took the curricle out on to the Cambridge road. But after ten minutes he had fallen silent once more and slouched in his seat, his eyes on the horses as they clip-clopped along the empty road.

'What are we going to do?' he asked.

'I don't know,' Richard said. 'Not yet, at least.'

The question of settling Jeffery's debts was the least of the problems. Sir Robert Standish was not a pauper, and he could find the money without much difficulty. Even if he could not, the Careys would, for they had a strong sense of family kinship, and they would never allow one of Aunt Anne's children to run into difficulties.

The trouble would be Uncle Robert's reaction to the news, and Richard frowned at his horses and shook them into a faster pace. He couldn't blame Uncle Robert, he decided; Jeffery had been pathetically stupid. Was there a chance of raising the money without Sir Robert ever learning what had happened?

Jeffery's elder brother William? Richard shook his head. William was in the Foot Guards and would need all his settlement; no hope of his raising five thousand.

Lord Aubigny? Richard dismissed the idea immediately. His father's sense of propriety would never allow him to settle Jeffery's debts without telling Uncle Robert.

The curricle pulled up with a violent jerk. 'Rupert!' Richard said. 'Uncle Rupert! The very man!'

'Rupert!' Jeffery said. 'Would he help? He'll have to tell Father, though.'

'Oh, no, he won't,' Richard said confidently. 'Not if I know Rupert.'

He grinned as he thought of his uncle, that wiry, impetuous little man, living like a nabob now on the Gower coast, not far from Llanstephan, after his career with the East India Company. Rupert was rich and generous. He would find the money, and what was better, he would do so with a childish delight behind the backs of Lord Aubigny and Sir Robert. He regarded them both with an amused contempt as stay-at-home politicians, while he had helped to build up an Empire in the East. And he had never really forgiven either of them for not voting against the trial of Warren Hastings, who together with Lord Clive was about the only man Richard had heard him praise unreservedly.

'Can you hold off those money-lenders for a few weeks?' Richard asked.

'I expect so. They'll wait if they think the money's on its way.'

'Right! Term ends next week. Father and Mother are in London until the end of the month, and I'm joining them there. You come with me, and with any luck we might find Rupert in town too. If not, you come to Llanstephan with us, and we'll drive over to Horton and tell Rupert the whole story.'

He twitched the reins, flicked his long whip with a carefree flourish, and the curricle went bouncing and rattling towards Cambridge.

Eight days later they were standing outside the Bull Inn waiting for Richard's groom to bring out the curricle, as their heavier baggage had already been sent on to London.

Richard was looking up at the sky and wondering how long it would be before the rain started, for heavy clouds were drifting up from the west; they would need their cloaks handy, he decided, as he heard a cheerful toot from a horn, and the London-bound stage-coach swung into the yard.

Richard and Jeffery strolled over to watch, for these crack services had reduced the change of horses to a fine art in an attempt to maintain their boasted ten miles an hour including stops. Several other undergraduates were there, one with a watch in his hand to time the change.

The fresh team of four Cleveland Bays was already harnessed and ready, and as two ostlers walked out the old team, the new one was pushed into place without any delay. High up on the front seat the coachman had dropped his reins and was leaning down for a tankard of beer, while the guard was hustling an old lady inside the coach as politely as he could, torn between his desire for a good tip and his anxiety to keep to the strict timetable.

'Yes, lady, five hours to London,' he said. 'Fastest and safest service on the road, lady. No, your bag will be perfectly safe in the boot. I'll keep my eyes on it personal.'

He swung up the steps, slammed the door and darted round to the boot, into which he hurled the lady's bag.

'All aboard!' he yelled.

The coachman was dealing with the beer; he could hardly be said to be drinking it, for as Richard watched him, he poured it down his throat, winked at Richard, threw the tankard to the ostler and picked up the reins. The ostlers holding the new team jumped to one side; the guard had scrambled up to his seat at the back, and then raised the horn to his mouth. The horses leapt forward, and with a practised skill that made Richard nod his head, the heavy vehicle swung round and through the narrow opening from the inn out on to the Trumpington Road.

'Two minutes and fifty seconds, Carey,' the undergraduate with the watch said. 'And you're going to meet some rain before you see London.'

'Afraid so,' Richard said. 'Here we are, Jeffery, up with you.'

They changed horses at the Red Lion in Royston and trotted on steadily towards Hoddesdon, stopping only at the various toll-gates to pay their way. Jeffery was reading Richard's copy of Patterson's *New and Accurate Description of all the Principal Roads in England and Wales*, for it contained a full list of inns, besides places where horses could be changed and the times of the main coaching services.

'What about the Saracen at Ware?' he suggested.

'Yes, the food's good there,' Richard said, 'and here's the rain.'

He stopped at the side of the road, and they struggled into their driving-capes just as the first drops of rain pattered on their tall beaver hats. A mile farther on they met a stage-coach, the outside passengers huddled up miserably on their exposed seats with the heavy rain lashing into their faces, and wishing no doubt that they had paid the higher price demanded for the inside seats.

Richard was glad to see the first buildings of Ware, and the welcome sight of the Saracen Hotel and an ostler who came running out to hold the horses. As they shook out their dripping cloaks in the hall, an attentive innkeeper bowed and offered Richard the bill of fare, with all the deference and respect that Richard expected and enjoyed, though he was not perhaps fully conscious of that fact.

They drove through several more showers before they reached London and the thicker traffic around Islington. From there the curricle was slowed to just over a walking pace until Richard swung into the comparative calm of Berkeley Square and drew up alongside the pavement and the front door of his father's house.

'His lordship is in the library, Mr Richard,' the footman said as he took their capes. 'Her ladyship is out but is expected home shortly.'

Richard led the way up the stairs and laid a warning hand on Jeffery's arm. 'Keep your mouth shut and your face still,' he said. 'You know Father; he can see through a brick wall farther than most people in London.'

Lord Aubigny was writing at the desk near the window as they were shown in, and he rose slowly to his feet and smiled at them both.

'Ah, Richard,' he said, and he held out his hand. 'And Jeffery, too. A good term, I trust. Your father and mother are down at Newton, Jeffery, but I hope you will stay here tonight.'

Lord Aubigny was in his late fifties, a slow-moving man, a trifle on the portly side now, and with his somewhat high-pitched but pleasant voice and his charming manners he frequently led strangers to believe that he was nothing more than an extremely rich nobleman whose chief interests were his own comfort and enjoyment. But as Richard and many others knew, those placid and plump features concealed a remarkable intelligence and a brain that moved with astonishing speed. Perhaps too quick, some of his friends thought, for he had no patience with dull or stupid people, and never concealed the fact. Probably that failing and an acid tongue had prevented him from reaching an even higher position in the Government.

As they all sat down again, and a footman carried round wine and biscuits, Lord Aubigny chatted casually about the latest political news in London. Richard made intelligent replies, and Jeffery wisely left the conversation to him.

'By the way,' the Earl said. 'Young Peter and Christopher will be glad to see you both. They are up in the nursery.'

'I'll go up in a moment,' Richard said, for he was fond of his cousin Henry's children. 'Henry is still in Calcutta, sir?' he asked.

'Yes. He is hoping to be in England next year.'

Richard nibbled a biscuit and prepared himself as casually as he could for the next question. The children were grandchildren of Uncle Rupert and lived with him while their parents were in India.

'Does that mean that Rupert is in London, sir?' he asked.

'No, he's in Italy.'

'Italy!' Despite his care, Richard had sat up quickly. From Jeffery there had come a stifled exclamation of dismay.

'Yes, in Rome by this time, I expect,' the Earl said. His eyes rested for a moment on Richard's face and then turned slowly to examine Jeffery, though without any apparent interest. But Richard knew his father. They had made a bad mistake, and he tried to cover it up as best he could.

'I suppose Rupert still detests a winter in England, sir,' he said, and refilled his glass.

'After the years he spent in India I don't suppose he will ever be warm enough here,' the Earl said. 'And goodness knows he keeps Horton hot enough with those enormous fires in every room.' He smiled at Richard and gently raised one eyebrow in inquiry.

Richard shrugged his shoulders. They might as well throw in the towel now, he decided. His father knew there was something amiss, and he was paying his son the compliment of showing him without unnecessary explanations that he was fully aware of the fact. Now that Rupert, their last hope, was out of England, the whole story would have to come out.

'You look pretty damp, Jeffery,' he said. 'Go up and change, and I'll meet you in the nursery with the two boys.'

Jeffery hesitated, but he took the hint, and as he shut the door behind him, Richard stood up and placed the silver tray of biscuits on a side table. The action gave him a little more time to decide what to say, but his father never believed in wasting time and came straight to the point.

'You were both very disappointed to hear that Rupert was out of England,' he said.

'Yes, we were, sir,' Richard said, leaning against the desk.

'I presume you needed his help in some matter. Rupert is an extremely resourceful man, and a rich one, too,' Lord Aubigny added significantly, and Richard, despite his uneasiness, could not help grinning. His father could certainly see the point of anything with remarkable speed.

'But why not come to me?' the Earl asked. 'Surely you know by this time that I should never refuse to help you, Richard. I did credit you with more intelligence and perception. Or perhaps I have given you the wrong impression as your father. If so, then the fault is mine, and I . . .'

Richard moved uneasily, 'No, no, sir,' he said. 'I'm sorry if you think that. If I ever needed help I should come to you immediately.'

'I'm very glad to hear that,' the Earl said, and he smiled at Richard. 'Then it's Jeffery who is in trouble. I half guessed as much. Money-lenders?'

Richard laughed. 'You are very quick, sir. How did you guess?'

'I didn't. I have heard rumours. Is it very serious?'

Richard nodded glumly. 'He's cleaned out, sir, and he owes about five thousand, I think.'

The Earl was as startled and dismayed as he ever allowed himself to be, but before he could say any more, the door opened and Lady Aubigny rustled into the room, a resplendent and striking figure, as she well knew, in a straw-coloured satin gown and one of the largest hats that Richard had ever seen, adorned with ostrich feathers. He smiled and bowed, for he was very fond of his mother, as indeed was everyone who knew her. Charming, completely frivolous, with unlimited generosity and kindness, she was incapable of saying a harsh word about a soul.

'You both look very serious,' she said. 'Richard dear, please remove this ridiculous hat immediately. I bought it this morning, and I cannot conceive why. Is it not utterly hideous?'

'Not at all, Mother. I thought it was charming.'

His mother chuckled. 'I wish you would pay compliments like that to all the girls we entertain in this house for your benefit.'

'For my benefit?' Richard grinned at her. 'My dear Mother, I don't want to get married yet.'

'Indeed not,' Lady Aubigny said decisively. 'I haven't found anyone suitable yet. Now, George,' and she turned to the Earl. 'Is Richard in trouble? Not sent down, Richard?' she exclaimed in alarm. 'The last Carey at Cambridge was sent down. Poor Alan! Mixed up in some stupid duel, and then went and buried himself in America. Really, my dear Richard, I don't want you to go rushing off to America. And certainly not India. George, you promise me you will not send Richard . . .'

She stopped as she saw them both laughing, and Richard put his hand on her arm. 'I'm not in trouble, Mother,' he said, 'and I haven't the slightest intention of taking the first ship to America or Calcutta. It's Jeffery,' and he explained the position.

'Poor Anne!' Lady Aubigny said. 'And poor Robert, too. He will explode.'

'He will, indeed,' the Earl said. 'I suppose you were going to ask Rupert to settle this without anyone knowing, eh, Richard?'

'I'm afraid so, sir,' Richard admitted. 'It sounded a wonderful idea last week, but I don't think much of it now.'

The Earl shook his head. 'No, it wouldn't have done, Richard, believe me. Jeffery must face the consequences sometime, and the sooner the better. You take him down to Newton in the morning and see what you can do to help.'

'Precious little,' Richard said. 'You know what Uncle Robert thinks of gambling?'

'I do. Jeffery should have thought about that too. Now, go up and see the boys. I promised them you would visit the nursery as soon as you arrived.'

In the nursery at the top of the house, a large, untidy and comfortable room in which Richard had spent many hours himself, he found his two young relations, eleven-year-old Peter, vigorous and noisy, and fair-haired Christopher, not yet four, sitting quietly in one corner, absorbed in a pile of wooden bricks and two lines of toy soldiers.

Peter greeted Richard with a whoop and hurled himself across the room. 'Uncle Richard! Come and look at this model frigate! And will you take me out in your curricle in the morning?'

'Sorry, Peter, but I've got to drive Uncle Jeffery down to Newton.'

'But you've only just come, Uncle Richard!' Peter looked reproachfully at his uncle. Grown-ups, he decided, were the most unreasonable people.

'Don't worry. You're both coming down to Llanstephan next week, and we'll go sailing.' He led the pacified Peter across the room, and they knelt down by the model ship. Christopher glanced up, smiled sweetly at his uncle, who ruffled his hair, and returned to his line of soldiers, moving them carefully into the fort he was building.

'Are you sure that foremast is in the right place?' Richard asked, picking up the model.

'Of course it is, Uncle!' Peter looked with disgust at Richard. 'I ought to know. I'm going into the Navy in three years. And, anyway, it's not the foremast. It's the mizzen. Don't you know that much about a ship?' he asked with withering contempt.

Jeffery, who had just come into the room, choked down his amusement. There were many young men at Cambridge who had writhed under Richard's tongue who would have given a large part of their monthly allowances to have overheard that rebuke.

Richard grinned. 'I'm afraid I don't know as much as you do about ships, Peter,' he said. 'You tell me,' he added meekly. He knelt there patiently and listened to the lecture, helped Christopher to add a court-yard to the fort, and only left the children when their nurse came to collect them. There was more than one side to Richard, Jeffery thought as they went to their rooms to dress for dinner.

Newton House, Jeffery's home, was some sixty miles or so to the west of London, and they arrived there in the middle of the afternoon. Jeffery, as might have been expected, became gloomier with each mile. His mood, as Richard noticed with dismay, was changing from one of shock and hor-ror at his losses to a feeling that he was a much-wronged and unfortunate young man, and that the world had treated him with great injustice. The trouble, as Richard thought uneasily, would be that Jeffery would include Uncle Robert with those who had been responsible; the slightest rebuke, and Jeffery would react with all the quick temper and obstinacy he possessed.

As they drove through the lodge gates and slowed down before the front entrance, Richard saw Lady Standish walking across the lawns towards them, and he reined in his horses. A groom came out from the stable, and led the curricle away while Lady Standish greeted her son.

But one look at his face was enough for her; she possessed much of her brother's quick intelligence. 'Trouble, Jeffery?' she asked.

'Yes, Mother. Bad trouble.'

'Oh, Jeffery.' She put one hand to her mouth. 'Your father is in the gun-room, I think. I should get it over quickly, Jeffery.'

She took Richard by the arm, and they walked across the grass to a small summer-house. She was trembling, and Richard patted her arm.

'Tell me, Richard,' she said, and she listened to the pitiful tale in silence until he had finished.

'It's very odd how memories come back to you, Richard,' she said. 'I can remember so well the look on my brother Alan's face when he arrived at Llanstephan after he had been sent down from Cambridge. And that must be twenty-five years ago.'

'And how did Grandfather deal with that, Aunt Anne?' Richard asked. 'He was a pretty formidable old fellow, wasn't he?'

'Oh, not really, Richard,' his aunt said. 'He could be very understanding.'

'And what about Uncle Robert?' Richard asked.

Lady Standish frowned. 'He may understand,' she said. 'But he will find it difficult to forgive. Jeffery has been very foolish, you know, Richard.'

'He has indeed,' Richard said. 'But it's not much use telling him so. Or is it? I don't know.' He fumbled in the side pocket of his riding-coat. 'I forgot to tell you, Aunt, but Father gave me letters for you and Uncle Robert. If there is anything he can do to help, with money, or in any other way . . .'

His aunt took the letters and smiled. 'We may need his help,' she said. 'Now go and change for dinner, Richard. But I'm afraid it may not be a very cheerful meal.'

Richard dressed himself carefully in a black coat, black silk knee-breeches and white stockings, and went down to the drawing-room. His uncle and aunt, together with Jeffery, were already there, a silent and gloomy little group. Richard glanced quickly at his cousin; Jeffery was flushed and sullen, and when he saw Richard's eyes on him he shrugged his shoulders angrily.

Richard sighed, and turned to his uncle. Sir Robert Standish was a somewhat austere-looking man, and Richard had never seen him in such a forbidding mood. His uncle, as he knew, could be charming, kind-hearted and generous, but his mouth was tight now, and his eyes frosty. Nevertheless he greeted Richard in a friendly fashion.

'It was kind of you to come down with Jeffery,' he said, 'and to bring your father's letter. But dinner is ready, and we will discuss all that later.'

Dinner, as Lady Standish had forecast, was not a cheerful meal, though the food and wine were as excellent as ever. Jeffery said little; he pecked at his food, and he emptied his wine-glass frequently.

A footman was lighting the candles in the drawing-room when they returned there, and Sir Robert took his place in front of the empty fire-place. He waited for them to sit down, and cleared his throat. Here we go, Richard thought, and braced himself for the worst.

'Your father has made an excellent suggestion, Richard,' he said.

'Oh yes, sir?' Richard was not surprised. The Earl invariably made excellent suggestions.

'Yes. He will use his influence with the East India Company to find Jeffery a post in Bengal or Madras. Your Uncle Rupert will also support this, and there should not be any difficulty.'

'India,' Richard said tentatively. He thought this was indeed an excellent suggestion, and he looked at Jeffery.

But Jeffery said nothing. He was staring sullenly at the pattern of the wallpaper immediately in front of him. Obviously he had very different ideas about the plan. Sir Robert glanced at his son, cleared his throat again and announced that he had letters to write in his study. Lady Standish hesitated, and with an anxious face followed her husband out of the room.

Richard lounged in his chair and wondered what he should say. He heard the clink of glass and watched Jeffery pour out his third glass of port.

'Can you lend me a hundred pounds, Richard?' he demanded.

Richard sat up. 'What?'

'Well, make it fifty; that should be enough.'

'Enough for what?'

Jeffery drank thirstily and reached out for the decanter. 'More port, Richard?'

'No, I've had enough, and so have you.'

Jeffery laughed and filled his glass. 'I'm not going to India,' he said.

'Why not?' Richard asked mildly. 'Uncle Rupert and Henry have done very well for themselves out there.'

'The glamour of the East, I suppose,' Jeffery said bitterly. 'Not for *me*,

Richard. Can you imagine me a writer with John Company? Sitting in a dusty office in Calcutta entering the price of pepper in a ledger?'

'Better than sitting in Naylor's losing thousands of pounds.'

Jeffery scowled at his cousin. 'Now, don't you start lecturing me,' he said. 'I've had enough of that from Father.'

'What did you expect him to say?' Richard said. 'You've lost all your money and cost him another five thousand.'

Jeffery snorted.

'Oh, all right, then I won't say any more,' Richard added hastily. 'But if you're not going to India, what are you going to do? And why the fifty pounds?'

'I'm going to France or Germany.'

'In heaven's name, why there?'

'I met some friends of Rupert's in London last year,' Jeffery said.

Richard groaned. 'His friends are a pretty mixed bag,' he said.

'Perhaps they are. Anyway, one of them was a Baron de Batz. He seemed to take a liking to me and gave me his Paris address, and one in Bavaria. He knew I was losing more than I could afford, and he told me if I wanted to make a fresh start, then I should get in touch with him.'

'And you want fifty pounds to travel?'

'Yes. Can you manage it?'

'I suppose so,' Richard said reluctantly. 'I'll have to give you a draft on my bankers.'

Jeffery smiled for the first time that evening, but Richard held up his hand. 'Now, wait, Jeffery. If I do, Uncle Robert will never speak to me again.'

'Who's going to tell him? I won't. I'll pay you back sometime, Richard, I really will. How can I ever thank you?'

'Don't try,' Richard said wearily. 'This is the stupidest thing I've ever done. And I'm going to bed. I shall probably have a nightmare of you begging for bread in the streets of Paris.'

He went out into the hall, picked up a candle from the side table there, and walked slowly up to his room.

3

News from France

Richard's last year at Cambridge passed slowly. He missed Jeffery far more than he had expected, for his cousin was one of the few friends with whom he had felt wholly at his ease. To fill the gap he read widely, to the surprise of his acquaintances, and he spent a considerable amount of time learning French and improving his fencing.

Capable tutors for both these subjects were easy to find in England now, for the number of French noblemen who were emigrating was increasing every month, and one of them, a man called de Lessart, had settled in Cambridge.

He was a very fine swordsman, and for most of the year Richard had fenced with him almost daily. Duelling was becoming a thing of the past, and there were few great swordsmen left outside the professional fencing masters, or so Lord Aubigny said. Richard was reasonable, his father admitted reluctantly, and he had improved with his many lessons. But he had not fenced with de Lessart much recently; the Frenchman had apparently lost interest or, more probably, as Richard thought, his skill was failing him, for he was no match for his pupil now.

One morning, a few weeks before the end of term, Richard turned in at the gates of Clare. The porter nodded to him and handed him a letter as he passed the lodge. Richard looked eagerly at the writing on the outside; it was from his father, and he pushed it into his pocket as he crossed the court towards his rooms. There was no need now to keep a look-out for the nervous and persistent Mr Bellamy, for that earnest and annoying young man had gone down, and was now presumably buried in his father's offices in London.

As he sat down and broke the seal of his father's letter, Richard wondered what Jeffery was doing at that moment; he had hoped that the letter might have been from him, for only two letters had arrived during the last year, and both from Bavaria. Rupert's mysterious friend, the Baron de Batz, had kept his promise, and Jeffery was with him, though he was extremely vague about his life, or how he was managing to live at all.

Richard sighed and opened his father's letter. It was short, and to the point.

> London, 1 June 1792
>
> My dear Richard,
>
> As you see, I am still in London, and have not yet left for Llanstephan, though I had hoped to leave two days ago. Join me here immediately. I have received disturbing news from France. Obtain leave of absence from your tutor, and tell him that you will not be returning this term.
>
> Your affectionate father,
> Aubigny

Richard arrived in Berkeley Square late the following afternoon and found his parents in the library.

'It's Jeffery, I suppose, sir?' he asked when they had exchanged greetings.

'Jeffery!' his father said in surprise. 'No, I'm afraid not, Richard. Nothing has been heard of him for six months. My news is from Normandy. Quentin d'Assailly has been arrested in Paris.'

'Oh, I see,' Richard said a trifle flatly. Quentin d'Assailly was the Marquis de Vernaye, the head of the French side of the family, but Richard had not seen him for years and had only the faintest recollection of his appearance. 'What are the charges, sir?' he asked.

'Charges!' the Earl said bitterly. 'Charges have little meaning in Paris at the moment. A revolutionary Government with its back to the wall, fighting a losing war against two of the strongest military Powers in Europe, has no time for legalities. Anyone who is suspected of being against it is liable to arrest. The prisons in Paris are full of people like Quentin.'

'But is there any immediate danger, sir?'

'Not at the moment. But if the Allies, the Prussians and the Austrians, march any closer to Paris, then Quentin's life won't be worth one of those assignats they are issuing so wildly.'

Richard went over in his mind the news from France that he had been reading in the newspapers.

'Is there any danger that the French Government will fall soon?' he asked.

'That is what we would all like to know,' the Earl said. 'The Allies are slow to move; they've wasted months now, and that may give the French time, and that's what they need most.'

'How badly disorganized is the French army, sir? They must have lost all their officers and generals when they emigrated.'

'That's true enough. But they have some very able men in power now. But if things go wrong, then they will turn on all their enemies at home. The King will probably be the first victim.'

Richard laughed. 'Oh, surely not, sir! This is France after all, a civilized country.'

The Earl looked pityingly at his son. 'You can forget all your ideas about civilization, Richard. These new men in Paris are desperate; if they lose the war, they lose their lives. Believe me, they will think nothing of slaughtering every prisoner in their hands before they go down themselves.'

Richard rubbed his chin. His father should know, he thought, with all the various sources of information open to a member of the Government.

'But surely some of these stories we hear are exaggerated?' he said doubtfully.

'I wish they were. Tomorrow you can talk with a man who has just left Paris. He's seen the mob there at work. If he told you all he knew you would be physically sick.'

'Please, George,' Lady Aubigny said.

'I'm sorry, my dear,' the Earl said. 'But Richard must realize the danger.'

Richard looked sharply at his father. They were at last coming to the point and the reason for that urgent summons from Cambridge. 'Where do I come into this, sir?' he asked.

'Amélie d'Assailly and the two children are still at Vernaye in Normandy. I want you to go over and bring them to England.'

'But, sir . . .' Richard started again. 'Surely they can just come of their own accord.'

'Not without passports, and they won't be given those. They will have to be smuggled out of the country.'

Richard spread out his hands helplessly. 'Since when have I been a professional smuggler?' he asked plaintively.

The Earl smiled and rolled out a map on his desk. 'Come here, Richard. Vernaye is just over three miles from the shore, near this little fishing village, Graye-sur-Mer, there,' and his finger stabbed at the map. 'A mile out of the village is a long, sandy beach. I know it well; Quentin and I used to ride there. You will be landed at night on that beach. You'll walk inland to the château, bring them all down to the beach, and then you sail away.'

'And they will all live happily ever after,' Richard said. 'You'll forgive my saying so, sir, but this is not your usual practice.'

The Earl laughed. 'Oh, I'm no man of action,' he said. 'The plan is Rupert's.'

'I might have known!' Richard exclaimed.

'It really is not so mad as it sounds,' the Earl said. 'It has the merit of being simple and direct. By my normal standards Rupert may talk a trifle wildly, but he has had much experience of action, and he has frequently said that the best plans are the simplest ones.'

'It still sounds crazy to me,' Richard said. 'How does Rupert propose to land me on this beach? Do I swim, or float gently down from heaven like a snowflake? Or perhaps Rupert has sent for some outlandish craft from India, and I dash ashore mounted on an elephant?'

'Simplicity, my dear Richard, is the keynote of the plan. Rupert will send you across the Channel with some smugglers of his acquaintance.'

'Trust Rupert to have his own private smugglers,' Richard said. 'I always wondered where his brandy came from. Is that how he buys it?'

The Earl smiled. 'I am a Justice of the Peace,' he said. 'I never ask my brother awkward questions. Anyway, the brandy is far too good; I merely drink it, and refill my glass.'

Richard looked up at his father and grinned. 'You shock me profoundly, sir,' he said. 'I suppose I must raise no more objections. Rupert obviously has everything ready.'

'Naturally.' The Earl's face became slightly worried, and he looked searchingly at his son lounging in his chair. 'Will you go, Richard? It might be dangerous.'

'Oh, I'll go,' Richard said without any hesitation. 'I wouldn't miss this for a year's allowance.'

The Earl nodded; his face had cleared. 'Tomorrow I want you to meet that Frenchman I told you about. The Vicomte de Marillac. He knows the Normandy coast, and as he was in France until quite recently, he can give you some useful advice. The next morning you leave for Wales. Rupert is expecting you, and he will do the rest. I can give you detailed instructions about the route from the beach to the Château de Vernaye.'

Richard went to bed in a mood of eager anticipation. The next few months promised to be interesting. He would be back in a couple of weeks from this caper in France, and after that he could go with Rupert on the continental tour that they had planned some time ago. The Mediterranean and Italy, Rupert had said, and as he had travelled widely there, he could show Richard the more unusual places, and introduce him to the extremely varied circle of friends he had made, for Rupert possessed a genius for collecting friends.

Early the next morning Richard went with his father to one of the Earl's clubs, and there they found the Vicomte de Marillac, a slim and youthful-looking man, dark, graceful and charming. Intelligent, too, Richard thought, and not as young as he appeared at first sight – probably in his thirties at least.

In an upstairs card-room, empty now, they discussed Richard's visit to France. Richard could not think of any particular information he might need, for he was not going more than a few miles inland, and then only for a couple of days at the most. But he did ask about local conditions in Normandy, the attitude of the ordinary people, their opinion of great families like the Assaillys.

'In general the great landowners are unpopular,' the Vicomte said. 'But that varies from district to district. The Assaillys were good landlords, so I expect they have been left alone.'

'And if I am seen landing?' Richard asked. 'Would anyone in the village ask awkward questions, or arrest me?'

De Marillac pursed his lips. 'Possibly, Monsieur Carey. If there is an active Republican in Graye-sur-Mer, for instance, then you would be in danger. I advise you to keep well clear of houses.' He spread out his hands expressively. 'Take no chances, *monsieur*.'

There did not seem much more information of value to be obtained from the Frenchman, and in any case, Richard thought that everyone was making an unnecessary fuss about the whole business. He might be plunging into the centre of unknown and primitive Africa instead of paying a short visit to the most civilized country in Europe.

The Earl had left for Whitehall, and Richard decided to spend the rest of the morning at Loubet's fencing academy. The afternoon could be spent at his tailor and bootmaker; he would need some new clothes before his journey to the Mediterranean with Rupert.

Loubet had no pupil when Richard climbed the stairs to the fencing gallery, and he was greeted with gratifying politeness, due not only to his rank and wealth, but also to the fact that Loubet considered him to be one of his most promising pupils.

They dressed themselves in the thickly padded vests and the wire masks used for safety, and Richard carefully picked a foil. A bout with Loubet would be interesting, he thought, after his many practices with de Lessart in Cambridge.

They both went through the graceful motions of the salute, and fell on guard for a second before Loubet attacked. Richard broke up a series of thrusts delivered with astonishing speed; Loubet's finger-play was so fine that he could switch from one line of attack to the other with an ease and deadly precision that would have overwhelmed the average swordsman.

But Richard remained cool. His technique had always been good, and those daily bouts with such an experienced fencer as de Lessart had given him an additional sense of timing, a split-second feeling of anticipation. He parried a thrust in carte with a rising thrill of self-confidence, and with a wonderful feeling that he had seconds to spare; so prompt and instinctive had been his parry that he was able to disengage and lunge in sixte. Loubet parried, but that thrust had nearly passed through his guard.

Richard increased his pressure, and it was Loubet now who was spending most of his time on the defensive. The great fencing master, Richard thought, was not a young man; he had probably been fencing with pupils all morning, and was tired. He had certainly lost much of his speed and anticipation. And he was weak against a thrust in sixte, Richard's brain told him.

The foils clashed and tinkled metallically, and a furious bout suddenly ended with Richard's long arm at full length, and behind it the six feet of his height. Loubet leapt to one side.

'*Touché!*' he called sharply, one hand to his chest where Richard's foil had gone home. He was staring at Richard through his mask. 'Again, Monsieur Carey?' he asked in his harsh voice.

Richard nodded, and once more they came on guard, and the bare room was filled with the stamp of feet, the grunts of two men at full stretch, and the clash of their foils. Loubet's assistant was no longer leaning against the wall with the bored attention of a man who sees too much of fencing. Instead he was watching with twitching hands, as if he was holding a foil, and he was muttering in French under his breath.

'*Touché!*' Richard called, and pointed to his left shoulder. 'Again, Loubet?' he asked.

He had been careless, he knew, trying a risky stop thrust against Loubet. He would take no chances this time, but fence as if there was no blunt tip to the foil and a mistake would cost him a thrust through the lungs. He fought with tremendous concentration, making the most of his greater height and reach. Loubet was watching that thrust in sixte; Richard tightened his lips, feinted in sixte, flicked his foil over, and forward went his right foot and his long arm in a lunge that bent the thin blade of the foil in a curve as the tip rammed against Loubet's chest.

Loubet tore off his mask; his dark face was flushed with exertion and annoyance, but he was deeply puzzled, too.

'With whom have you been fencing, Monsieur Carey?' he asked.

'Oh, with an *émigré* in Cambridge,' Richard said. 'The Vicomte de Lessart. But he has become very slow, you know, Loubet. He is not so young as he was.'

'De Lessart?' Loubet said, and he exchanged glances with his assistant. 'Henri de Lessart?'

Richard nodded. 'Yes, that's the man.' He was stripping off his vest, and Loubet's assistant handed him his waistcoat. 'You let me off lightly this morning, Loubet. I expect you are tired after a busy morning with your other pupils.'

Loubet opened his mouth, and then bowed. 'But of course, *monsieur*,' he said. He helped Richard into his coat, accepted his fee – a generous one

– with another bow, and in silence waited for the door to close.

Then Loubet flung his mask against the wall with a crash, and exploded into a torrent of French and Italian oaths. His assistant tactfully said nothing, and waited for the storm to subside, when he would be able to make some soothing remarks.

'Tired!' Loubet exclaimed, the first coherent word that had emerged so far. 'Let him off lightly! Did you hear that, Etienne?'

'Yes, *monsieur*.'

'Me, Gaston Loubet, tired! And I have done no fencing this morning! De Lessart too slow! Not so young as he was! One of the finest swordsmen in France! Did you hear that?'

'Yes, *monsieur*.'

Loubet took a deep breath and clenched his hands as if to fight down another outburst. 'It is true', he said a little more quietly, 'that I may no longer have that superlative speed that once made me, Gaston Loubet, the greatest *maître d'armes* in Europe. After all, I am over sixty, am I not, Etienne?'

'But of course, *monsieur*,' said the assistant, who knew very well that Loubet was not a year older than fifty-two.

'But to be hit twice in as many minutes!' Loubet muttered sadly. 'Such a thing has not happened since last year, when I fought with Pietro Donelli in Rome. He hit me once in sixte. And I was suffering from a fever that day, as you will remember, Etienne.'

'But of course, *monsieur*,' and Etienne nodded his head vigorously. The great Loubet had certainly not been at his best, but four bottles of wine the night before had not improved his eye or his timing.

'Monsieur Carey is undoubtedly a fine swordsman,' Loubet admitted. 'His reach is phenomenal,' and he held out his own arms.

'Phenomenal,' said his tactful echo. 'And you taught him; he is your pupil, Monsieur Loubet.'

'That is so, Etienne. He is indeed my pupil,' Loubet said gratefully. 'And you must remember that his father was once a fine swordsman, and his grandfather was the most noted and dangerous duellist in Europe.'

Loubet was rubbing his hands with some satisfaction now. 'When I next meet Jules Didier, I can tell him that I have produced a finer swordsman than his favourite pupil, de Marillac.'

Etienne showed some sign of animation at last. 'I saw the Vicomte de Marillac in London yesterday, *monsieur*,' he said eagerly.

Loubet, who had moved across to the windows, spun round with all the grace and speed of the trained fencer. 'In London! Are you certain, Etienne?'

'But yes, *monsieur*. I would know him anywhere.'

Loubet turned back to the window again, one hand stroking his blue jowl. 'De Marillac in London,' he said slowly. 'Now, that I find most interesting,' he said, but he did not explain why. 'Ah, there goes Monsieur Carey. Possibly one of the three greatest swordsmen in Europe, and he does not know it!'

He suddenly pulled off his fencing vest. 'My coat, Etienne, and my hat, immediately. I have a call to make, and I shall not be back for at least an hour.'

4

Rupert Carey

Richard left London in his curricle soon after dawn the following morning. His father had impressed upon him the need for speed, and though Richard still regarded the whole business with some amusement, he fell in with the Earl's wishes. He should reach Gloucester before dark, he thought, and he would spend the night there.

He enjoyed the long drive. The day was fine and warm, he was fortunate in his changes of horses, and he rattled steadily westwards all day until he came over the brow of Birdlip Hill, and there below in the setting sun was the wide plain, the jumble of rooftops, and the towers of Gloucester Cathedral.

He put up at the Fleece, ate an enormous dinner, stretched his long legs

gratefully in a stroll afterwards, for sitting up in the high curricle for many hours had cramped him, and then went up to bed, leaving instructions for an early call, and a team of good horses to be ready for him at eight o'clock.

He was whistling cheerfully as he took the curricle over the Severn and along the familiar road to Chepstow. Another hundred miles of steady driving, and he would reach Rupert's house on the Gower coast in time for dinner.

He made his last change of horses at Swansea, where he was known, and the landlord gave him the best horses available. The curricle bumped

and lurched along the rough road up to Killay, but Richard was still whistling. He was near his home, and he could see the sea now to his left, with the sweep of Swansea Bay, and the soft lines of the Devon coast on the other side of the Channel.

The last few miles down the narrow and winding lanes to Horton were comparatively slow, and at last Richard swung through the lodge gates of Horton. He stretched his stiff legs and thought with longing of a cool drink, for the sun was hot.

A small figure in pantaloons, short coat and high collar came rushing towards him, one arm waving frantically. It was young Peter, and Richard reined in his horses as the boy scrambled up beside him.

'Hello, Uncle Richard. I've been waiting for hours for you. Can I take the reins?'

'No, you can't. A curricle is far too dangerous. How's Chris?'

'Oh, he's all right,' Peter said. 'Too young for me to play with. He's only four. I say, Uncle Richard, can I come with you to France?'

'Can you . . . no, you certainly can't. Who put that crazy idea into your head? Your grandfather?'

'It's my idea. After all, Uncle Richard, I shall be in the Navy in a few years. I wouldn't come ashore with you if you didn't want me. I could stay on board with Ianto Price.'

'You won't be coming at all. And who's Ianto Price?'

'He's a smuggler. He's taking you to Normandy. I go fishing with him. He's a friend of Grandfather's.'

'I bet he is,' Richard said, as he guided the curricle around the curve in the drive and stopped outside the front door of Horton Lodge, an old and sprawling house that Rupert had bought on his return from India, and which he had modernized considerably.

A tall, powerful man dressed as a butler came down the steps. This was Idwal Jones, who had been Rupert's servant for many years in the East. His language alternated between a mixture of English, Welsh and Hindustani and a wide choice of oaths in all three tongues. This was apparently one of his English days, for he greeted Richard in his stateliest manner.

'Good afternoon, Mr Carey,' he said, and bowed stiffly. 'Sir Rupert is in the library, sir. I trust you had a good journey from London, sir.'

Richard cocked a sardonic eye at him. 'You're devilish formal today, Idwal.'

'Well, it's a perishing butler I'm supposed to be, Mr Richard. And a perishing good one, Sir Rupert says, too.'

Richard coughed. 'Language in front of the children, Idwal,' he said reprovingly.

Idwal glanced at Peter, who had just passed them on the steps. 'He'll learn worse than that in the perishing Navy, Mr Richard. Takes after his grandfather. Regular young perisher.'

Richard shrugged his shoulders helplessly. The richness and variety of Idwal's oaths and unprintable adjectives never ceased. He went up the steps and into the white-panelled hall. Two logs smouldered in the fireplace despite the warm sunlight that came through the windows. But that was nothing unusual at Horton, where the temperature of the house was invariably kept at hot-house heat. Rupert frequently complained of the heat he had suffered in India, but he was equally critical of the English climate.

'*Koh hai! A-jao, jaldi!*' bellowed Idwal, and a footman ran into the hall. He must have learnt a good deal of Hindustani, Richard thought. 'Mr Richard's baggage from his curricle, Tom. Up to his room, *ek dum!*'

A door behind them opened, and a small, slight, wiry man in tight pantaloons, a brown coat and a violent yellow waistcoat bounced into the hall.

'Ah, there you are, Richard,' he said. 'Idwal, brandy, decanter and glasses!'

'Beer, if you don't mind, Rupert,' Richard said, for his uncle preferred to be called by his Christian name. 'My throat's full of dust.'

'Rotgut!' Sir Rupert said. 'Now, run away, Peter; I want to talk to Richard.'

'Uncle Richard says I can't go with him to France, Grandfather,' Peter said. 'Can't I? Ianto Price said I could.'

'Nothing to do with Ianto, my boy. Wait until you're in the Navy. You'll have plenty of excitement then.' Rupert swept Richard into the library, where another log fire was burning.

'Some fool opened the windows this morning,' Rupert said. 'Like a December blizzard blowing about my ears. Good boy, Peter. He'll do well in the Navy.'

'And Chris?' Richard asked.

'Quiet boy, Chris. Can wheedle his nurse into anything. Going to be a soldier, he says. Well, I can give him a few tips about soldiering.'

Idwal brought in a tray and decanters and a large tankard of beer, which Richard drained blissfully. Rupert was already pulling his chair close to the fire, his pointed and aggressive chin jutting out over the folds of his cravat. His face was dark and wrinkled, especially at the corner of each eye. He was nearly bald now, with twin tufts of grey hair shooting up above each ear, and between them was the smooth expanse of his scalp, as shiny and well polished as Richard's Hessian boots.

'When do Henry and Catherine come home?' Richard asked.

'Next month,' Rupert said. 'Henry doesn't want to go back again to Bengal. Good brain, you know, Richard, but no ambition. He'll never set the Carnatic on fire.'

Richard put up a hand to smother the smile on his lips. From all that he had heard and read, Rupert and his contemporaries had set far more than the Carnatic ablaze.

Rupert refilled his glass and ran his hard blue eyes over Richard, from the crown of his carefully brushed hair to the tips of his equally well-polished boots. It was difficult to tell whether or not he approved of what he saw.

'You know what you've got to do, eh?' he asked abruptly.

'Oh, yes, Rupert, but the whole affair sounds very melodramatic.'

Rupert grunted. 'Expect it does, my boy. You've led a very sheltered life until now.'

'Sheltered!' Richard put down his tankard and glared indignantly at his uncle.

But Rupert merely grinned. 'Before I'd reached your age, Richard, I'd fought at Plassey, and spent two weeks in a stinking dungeon belonging to the Nawab of Bengal, under sentence of death by being trampled on by an elephant. They took me out twice to watch it happen.'

He gulped down his brandy.

'You've lived soft, my boy,' he went on, ignoring Richard's angry stare. 'Money, good food, regiments of servants, and a pleasant and peaceable existence. You must learn how to do without all that, you know, some day.'

Richard was nettled, and by no means convinced. Rupert lived in the past, he thought, and the older he grew, the more exaggerated were his stories. But his uncle was reading his thoughts with surprising accuracy, and his blue eyes twinkled. He was a good judge of character; often his life had depended upon such a judgement, and Richard would do, he decided, once he received a few painful jolts to his complacency and his comfortable existence.

'Now, go and take those dusty clothes off,' he said, 'and we'll dine. In the morning we'll ride down to Port Eynon, and you can go aboard. Ianto is hoping to sail on the evening tide.'

'Tomorrow night!' Richard exclaimed, shocked by this indecent haste.

'Yes, of course!' Rupert snapped impatiently. 'When you've made your plan, you don't sit around admiring the polish on your boots, my boy. We didn't conquer Bengal like that!'

Richard groaned, but he knew from past experience that once Rupert took charge of affairs, then other people meekly did as they were told. The wiry little man had a way with him, as even Richard was forced to admit.

They ate their dinner in an overheated dining-room, with all the windows closed, and heavy curtains drawn across them, and a Chinese screen in front of the door to keep out the slightest draught. To his dismay Richard discovered that one of the many courses was a curried dish, and Rupert's curry, as Richard knew, was to be approached with caution. But under his uncle's baleful eye, he tried to finish what little he had put on his plate, while his eyes streamed and the perspiration trickled down his forehead.

Rupert ate with gusto, and gave his views on the political position in France, and what he would have done in the place of poor King Louis. The streets of Paris, so Richard gathered, would have been filled with guns if Rupert had been given command, and the cobbles covered with the corpses of the Paris mob.

'More curry, my boy?' he asked.

'No, I'm on fire already,' Richard said, and he wiped his forehead.

'Give him an ice, Idwal. Finest ices I've ever seen were in Rome,'

Rupert said, taking a large spoon and tackling his ice. 'Must take you there if the old boy is still alive.'

'Which old boy?'

'The Cardinal de Bernis, French Ambassador to the Papacy. Lives like a prince in the Palazzo de Carolis. Finest dinners in Europe,' Rupert declared emphatically, punctuating his sentences with mouthfuls of ice. 'Saw a Canon of St Peter eat fourteen ices in a row there one night. My favourite dish from his chef is a *queue d'agnerau à la Montauban*.' Another mouthful of ice and a short pause. 'Admired a model of Neptune made in marzipan on whipped cream waves one evening. Lackey called at my hotel next morning with it on a tray. Present from the Cardinal, he said. Idwal, more ices, and give one to Mr Richard. Found the curry too hot by the look of him.'

Richard did not refuse the ice. 'Did you eat Neptune in marzipan and the whipped cream waves, Rupert?'

'What the devil do you think I did with it?' Rupert demanded. 'Leave it in my rooms for some thieving hotel servant to guzzle?' He dug a spoon into his third ice. 'Whipped cream was off, though. Too hot in Rome.'

Richard shook with helpless laughter. The picture of Rupert sitting in his Rome hotel steadily working his way through an enormous figure of Neptune in marzipan was too much for him.

'The deuce take me if I can see anything amusing in that,' Rupert said in mild surprise. 'Now if I had said that I liked the model of the Colosseum in meringue that was standing on one of the side tables that night, then that would have been a different matter. A few spoonfuls of a well-cooked meringue is one thing, but the whole Colosseum, oh no,' and he shook his head and took another spoonful of ice.

'In meringue!' Richard exclaimed. 'Does the Cardinal de Bernis make a practice of sending his guests the contents of his cold buffet?'

'Invariably, my boy. Procession of lackeys in the Embassy livery down the Corso each morning. One of the regular sights of Rome.'

Richard decided that his journeys with Rupert would be extremely revealing. 'Where are you taking me after Rome?' he asked.

'Venice, and then on down the Dalmatian coast. Hire a well-found schooner in Venice, I think. Drop in on one of the Pashas I know in Albania. Interesting old fellow. Arranged a special execution for my benefit after dinner one night.'

Richard wiped his forehead again, and leant back in his chair. 'My dear, respected uncle,' he said, 'your ideas of an after-dinner entertainment!'

'Oh, I didn't approve, my boy,' Rupert said severely. 'There's a time and place for everything, including executions.'

The heat of the room was overpowering by this time, or perhaps it was the effect of the curry and the wine he had drunk, Richard thought. The panels of Chinese wallpaper on either side seemed delightfully cool, and he wished he could dive into the deep pools that were painted so delicately under the fantastically shaped bridges. Rupert, he noticed, was unmoved by the heat or the wine, though his face was a trifle redder, and his pink scalp had acquired an even glossier appearance. He was waiting now for Idwal to arrange three bowls of fruit in front of him, an exotic mass of colour that must have been imported for Rupert's benefit at great expense. For Rupert, as Richard knew, had acquired a taste for fruit in the East.

'A Jaffa orange, my boy?' Rupert said. 'Must take you to Palestine. Friend of mine there grows these.'

'I couldn't eat a thing more,' Richard said. He was longing for the coolness of the terrace outside. 'Anyway, I must go and pack if I'm sailing tomorrow evening.'

'Pack!' barked Rupert. He was tearing the peel from a huge orange. 'Where the devil do you think you're going? On the Grand Tour?'

'But I must take some clothes,' Richard protested.

'All you need is a sword and a pair of pistols. Or do you picture yourself tramping over the Normandy countryside in the middle of the night with a pile of baggage draped over your back like a damned pedlar?'

'I suppose not,' Richard said reluctantly. He would agree to anything if he could escape from this tropical heat.

'I spent three weeks on the Indian roads dressed as a beggar once,'

Rupert said. 'D'ye think I had a train of bearers behind a tree with fresh changes of clothes, or a valet to polish my boots for me? You must learn to rough it, my boy. I didn't have any boots on that time, incidentally,' he added, as he spat a mouthful of pips into a saucer.

Despite his discomfort Richard chuckled. Looking across the table littered with cut glass and lovely silver to his uncle resplendent in a plum-coloured coat, an attentive Idwal behind his back, it was difficult to picture Rupert huddled under a tree in the Indian forest, or trudging along barefoot in the dust of an Indian summer.

'But I'm going to France, not India, Rupert,' he said.

Rupert pushed away his plate and the remains of three oranges. 'You may not find much difference,' he said quietly.

Richard was startled by the sudden change in Rupert's tone of voice. For the first time a suspicion crept into his mind that this trip across the Channel might not be such a pleasure cruise as he had imagined.

'Must show you India one day,' Rupert said. 'Or send you out with some introductions. Go and live with the natives, that's the way to learn. You could stay with the Maharajah of Dunipore. He'll take you tiger-shooting. Do anything for me. Saved his life one day when he fell off his elephant and a tiger charged him.'

'What did you do about that, Rupert?' Richard asked curiously.

'Jumped down and shot the tiger, of course,' snapped Rupert. 'You've got some strange ideas, my boy. What in the name of fortune d'ye think I'd do?'

Richard shook his head. 'I'm going to bed,' he said.

'Half the port decanter left,' Rupert said reprovingly. 'Think I'd better come with you to Normandy, Richard.'

Richard staggered to his feet. 'Now, look here, Rupert,' he said. 'The last thing Father told me was to see that you stayed at Horton. He said that you would probably start an international incident within hours of landing in Normandy.'

Rupert grunted crossly. 'Bet you a thousand rupees, my boy, that you make a mess of this business,' he said belligerently.

'I don't know how much that is in guineas,' Richard said. 'But I'll take you, Rupert.'

Richard crossed the hall and opened the front door, walking slowly along the terrace in the blissful coolness of the night. The moon was up, nearly full, he noticed, which might be useful when this smuggler friend of Rupert's landed him on that beach in France.

It was very quiet on the terrace, and he could hear the low roar of the sea in the distance. The trees threw long black shadows across the lawns, and the fantastic world of Rupert with his tales of being trampled by elephants, or spending weeks disguised as a native, seemed very unreal and far away. But Rupert had lived an extraordinary life in the East; the trouble was that he seemed to think the same things could happen in Europe. Richard laughed, and went inside to find a candle.

They rode down to Port Eynon the next morning, and walked along the little quay towards a sloop moored there. Richard did not profess to know much about ships, apart from the occasional sailing he did at Llanstephan. But he could see for himself the scrubbed decks, the gleam of the brass-work, and the general air of tidiness and order.

Rupert strode over the gangway and jumped down nimbly to the deck. 'Ianto!' he shouted peremptorily.

A muffled voice replied, and a dark shock of hair appeared at a hatch-way, followed by a long, thin face the colour of teak, and six feet of a long, thin body dressed in clean duck trousers and a white shirt.

'*Duw*, man, I thought we should miss the morning tide,' he said to Rupert. 'This my passenger, sir?'

'This is my nephew, Mr Richard Carey,' Rupert said. 'And his baggage, though what he wants any for, I can't imagine.'

The luggage consisted of one tiny valise, the smallest Richard could find, and he proposed to leave that on the sloop when he landed. But there was no point in explaining, he decided.

'Remember you're bringing two ladies back with you, Ianto,' Rupert said.

'Yes, indeed,' Ianto said. 'The cabins be as clean as they always are, Sir Rupert, and you know what that's like.'

'Good. Well, good luck, Richard. Still think it would be safer if I came with you. But you might as well stand on your own feet for once.'

He shook hands briskly and stepped back on to the quay. Richard grinned and shook his head. Stand on his own feet, he thought wearily. Rupert must think he was a child.

Ianto began to shout orders in his high-pitched voice, and as Richard felt the deck sway and lift under his feet, he saw Rupert mounting and waving a hand before he trotted along the quay. Then the sloop heaved to the swell of the Bristol Channel, and a burst of spray made Richard duck his head and clutch at his hat.

5

The Château de Vernaye

The oil lamp that swung gently from the roof of the little cabin did not throw out a great deal of light. But there was enough for Richard to see what he was doing. He was carefully loading two pistols – not his own pair which his father had given him last year, but a pair of rifled screw-barrelled pistols that Rupert had insisted on pushing into his valise. Richard had not used screw-barrels before, though he was familiar with their design. They were no recent development; in the gun-room at Llanstephan there was a very old pair that Neil Carey had carried during the Civil Wars.

Richard unscrewed the long barrel and filled the patent breech with fine powder; then he balanced the bullet on the narrow tip of the breech and screwed down the barrel on to the bullet. He had heard the arguments for and against these screw-barrels. One of the disadvantages, he had been told, was that they were slow to reload, though he did not think so now. But no one had ever denied their astonishing accuracy and long range.

The patent breech compressed the explosion of the charge and gave a tremendous velocity to the bullet; the bullet was forced very tightly into the rifled barrel, and so would be rotated by the grooves. Richard gave a final turn to the barrel with the special wrench, and then held both pistols in his hands. They were heavy weapons, but the balance was good, and the smooth, well-shaped butts fell comfortably into the palms of his hands. He smiled; he would be extremely surprised if he used either on this short trip to France.

There was a tap on the cabin door, and a voice called, 'Ianto says we'll be inshore in an hour, Mr Carey.'

Richard called back, and stood up carefully, for the cabin was far too low to allow him to stand upright, and he had hit his head a shattering blow on the roof his first night aboard. He had selected his clothes with some care, and with the grudging approval of Rupert: an old riding-coat, his shabbiest coat and pantaloons, reserved for shooting in bad weather, a well-worn, low-brimmed hat and a pair of strong boots. Into the pocket of the coat he stuffed a pair of stockings, a clean shirt and his razor. The night might be cold, so he wound a silk scarf round his neck and was ready.

He looked regretfully at the valise on the floor with its changes of clothes; but Rupert was right, he could never carry that around with him. The odd thing was that Rupert seemed to be right about a good many matters, he was discovering. Finally he patted his waist, and could feel the heavy belt fastened round him; inside were a hundred gold sovereigns for use in an emergency, good currency anywhere in the world, and especially so in France, flooded now with too much paper money.

He made his way to the deck and stood by Ianto's tall figure. Ianto had suggested he should come on deck at least an hour before he was landed, so that his eyes could become accustomed to the darkness. Not that there was much to be seen, for the moon was hidden behind dark clouds, and only occasionally could Richard see tiny spots of light on the distant Normandy coast. The sloop was slipping easily over the calm sea, and Richard did not ask Ianto if he was certain that they were heading in the right direction. The sloop had made this trip before, and would do so again frequently, Richard guessed, and Rupert had warned him not to ask awkward questions. In any case, Ianto was being paid lavishly by the Carey family for this trip, and Rupert had promised him a further reward if the whole business was carried out successfully.

'Close enough,' Ianto said, and he passed low-voiced orders to his small crew. The sloop rose and fell gently on the swell, and Richard peered towards the land. He could see the irregular skyline now against the slightly greyer background, but that was all. It seemed ridiculous to him that Ianto could possibly have found his way to the exact beach in this light.

'I hope this is the right place, Ianto,' he said.

'*Duw*, man, this is the right beach. I've taken off many a good load of French brandy from here.'

His voice was confident enough for even Richard's sudden doubts, and without any more comments he followed Ianto over the side into the rowing-boat that one of the crew had lowered. A sword was not the easiest of weapons to manage when stepping into a small boat, but Richard finally found himself sitting beside Ianto in the stern.

'Shove off, Howell,' Ianto said, and they slid away from the sloop into the unwelcome darkness.

They must have been closer to the shore than Richard had realized, for in a very short time Howell was shipping his oars, and the boat ground on the sand.

'There you be, Mr Carey,' Ianto said. 'We'll be off here for the next three nights. Remember, three flashes with a lantern, wait, and then one more.'

'Right, Ianto.'

Richard stepped over the side into a foot of water, and splashed his way towards the firmer sand. He could hear the creak of the rowlocks behind him, but when he stopped and turned, he could see nothing, not even the sloop. He was completely alone at midnight on an unknown French beach, not even certain that it was the right beach. For the first time in his life he was really standing on his own feet. The secure foundations of family influence, money and position had all been knocked away, and he would have to rely on what natural talents he possessed. Something of this he realized, but not a great deal. All he knew was that this business might not, after all, be quite the holiday trip he had expected it to be.

As he trudged up the beach, slipping in the soft sand, he found himself wishing that he could hear Rupert's brisk and incisive voice. With a shock he learnt his second lesson, that his uncle was something more than an entertaining old character with his fantastic stories of life in India; he was a man of strong and violent action, a leader whom many other men had followed without hesitation.

There seemed to be a gap in the sand dunes ahead, and Richard swung to his right, climbed with some difficulty through the sand, and reached the top. There he lay down and wondered if the moon would come out. Both his father and Rupert had given him precise instructions about his next move, for this was the vital moment. If he took the wrong direction from the beach, then he would never reach Vernaye that night, and would have to move by day, asking for help from nearby villages. And that might well endanger the whole plan.

Richard went over the advice he had been given. 'Don't rush inland', Rupert had said, 'until you are certain of your bearings; a few minutes, even an hour's planning, is vital, before you start anything.'

The Earl, who knew the beach of Graye-sur-Mer, had told him to look out for one landmark inland: a solitary windmill that would stand out against the skyline. Make for that, he had said, and Richard would find a narrow lane which eventually passed one of the lodge gates of the Château de Vernaye.

Obediently Richard looked for the windmill. But he could see nothing, not a single dark shape that resembled a windmill. The first flicker of panic crept over him. Ianto had put him ashore on the wrong beach, after all. He might be twenty miles from Vernaye; the château might be to the west or the east, and he would be none the wiser. Or perhaps the windmill had been demolished; his father had not been here for ten years.

Richard drew a deep breath and tried to control his fears. Rupert had warned him about this, too. Think about something else, had been his advice. If you panic, you are lost.

Richard felt for the pistols; they were still there. He patted the belt at his waist; the sovereigns were there too, and they, surely, would get him out of trouble. Richard had found that money would solve most troubles. At least, it did in England; but would France be so obliging?

But before he could start worrying about that, the moon suddenly appeared, and the trees, the sand dunes and the fields all sprang into view as he lay there. And there, without any doubt at all, was the windmill, slightly to his left. The Earl had been right, and Ianto had performed the miracle of putting him ashore at exactly the right spot.

Richard jumped to his feet. He turned to look out to sea, but despite the moonlight, he could see no sign of the sloop on the flat, inky surface of the water. There was no comfort there, and Richard smiled ruefully. He knew now the meaning of the hackneyed saying that you could burn all your boats behind you. He could go forward, and nowhere else.

At the bottom of the sand dune he crossed a rough track and followed the line of a hedge that led towards the windmill. Five minutes later he was staring up at the great arms of the mill, and there in front of him was the lane that would take him to Vernaye, three miles away, so the Earl had said.

The lane was typical of the bocage country into which he was plunging, narrow, winding and shut in on either side by high banks and hedges that seemed even more forbidding in the darkness. He felt as if he was walking along a tunnel many feet below the earth, a tunnel, moreover, with a dreadful floor, deep ruts, sudden holes, that Richard could not possibly see in that bad light.

He stumbled on, now climbing, now dropping down a slope, the lane winding continually like a corkscrew. It was very quiet, too, and Richard could near nothing but the scuffling of his boots on the uneven ground. He stopped several times, though he was not quite certain what he did expect to hear. He was annoyed with himself for his nervousness, like a small boy afraid of the dark.

He must have walked for an hour, he thought, but there was no point in looking at his watch in the dark. Long ago he had come to detest this infernal lane, with its potholes and corners and high banks, an interminable tunnel that seemed to take him nowhere. He was sweating, too, inside the thick coat, and he tugged at the silk scarf around his neck. The heavy gold coins at his belt were dragging him down, and he was surprised to find how tired his legs were.

The hedge suddenly fell away, and the lane widened. To his left was a stone wall; this at last must be the park of the château. He quickened his pace, all his tiredness and doubts vanishing, and in five minutes he was looking up at two tall stone pillars on either side of the great entrance gates. But they were securely locked, and he thought it might be risky to knock up the people living in the lodge. Even that would take time, for he could see no lights in any of the windows.

He went ten yards or so before he came to part of the wall which had crumbled, and which he managed to climb, feeling extremely undignified, for he had not climbed like this since he was a boy. He put one long leg over the wall, then the other, and let himself down as best he could, hampered by the folds of his riding-coat. He dropped down to the turf, wiped the dirt from his hands fastidiously, and wondered when he would be able to wash himself.

Ahead was the drive leading to the château, flanked by an avenue of fine trees, throwing long, dense shadows in the moonlight. An owl hooted above his head, and the leaves of the trees rustled softly in the breeze. He thought, too, he could hear the murmur of the sea, but that might have been his imagination, for he felt tense and jumpy.

He started to walk up the avenue, keeping to the grass verge, his confidence returning now that he had reached the last stage of his journey. A good meal, a drink and a comfortable bed in the château, and then down to the beach where Ianto Price would be waiting for them. He laughed aloud. This would be a simple business, and old Rupert was nothing but an alarmist. The old boy would be sitting in front of one of his enormous fires at that moment, finishing the port decanter.

Richard was not far wrong, for far away on the other side of the Channel, Sir Rupert Carey was indeed sitting by his library fire, his head cocked to listen to the clip-clop of a tired horse trotting up the drive. He had acquired an instinctive sense of danger, and he did not like the sound of this late arrival. As Idwal brought him a letter, he saw that it was addressed in his brother's handwriting, and he opened it with misgiving.

Idwal stood there watching his master, and the telltale signs of the firm mouth tightening which he knew so well.

'Too late!' Rupert muttered. 'Can't do anything now. Damn it, we must! Idwal, tell them to saddle two horses! Send a footman for my riding-boots. We're riding to Swansea tonight!'

Richard was standing at the foot of one of the trees. The drive had turned, and there, about three hundred yards away, was the château, a long, low building, spanning the full width of the avenue, a vast white mansion with two lines of windows, and flanked at each end with round towers that rose to a sharply pointed roof like the snuffers on a candle-stand.

With a sigh of relief he hurried down the drive, not bothering now to conceal himself; this indeed was Vernaye, for he had seen engravings of it at Llanstephan. The closer he approached, the larger the château seemed to grow, with its wide façade of blank, shuttered windows, a greyish-white mass in the moonlight.

A slight feeling of uneasiness returned to him. There was not the slightest vestige of a light to be seen anywhere; the huge building was lifeless, still and ghostlike in the dark silence and the trees that surrounded it on every side. Richard hesitated. He did not like the look of all this. It was late, of course, nearly midnight, and the Assaillys and their servants would be asleep.

He swung to the right and went up a shallow flight of steps that led to a wide terrace. He went to the nearest window and tried to peer through the shutters, but he could see nothing. He glanced around nervously; he thought he had heard a footstep on the stone-flagged terrace, but there was nothing to be seen.

He tiptoed along the terrace, though he could have given no reason for his caution. Below the terrace was a large formal garden, a geometrical design of hedges and lawns and flower-beds, with a circular lily-pond in the centre. In one corner was a small summer-house with graceful columns, a fairy-tale picture in the moonlight. The whole place, in fact, reminded him of the illustrations in a book he had pored over as a child, the story of the sleeping princess and the quiet, lifeless palace in which she lived, where nothing moved, and time had come to a standstill.

Suddenly he halted. A thin shaft of light spilled out across the terrace and lit up a statue at the head of the stone steps leading down to the garden. Richard smiled. There was someone here, after all, and he hurried towards the window and put his face close to the shutters.

Feet clinked on the stone flags behind him. He whirled round. Against the dark sky he saw a raised arm, a bulky black figure, and then a stunning blow descended on his head, and the whole scene exploded in a flash of brilliant light, and he crumpled to the ground.

6

Armand d'Assailly

Richard opened his eyes and groaned. He felt sick, and his head was throbbing steadily. Lucky I was wearing a hat, was his first thought. He tried to move his arms and sit up, and then he thought he was in the middle of a dream where you try to run, and your arms and legs refuse to move.

But this was no dream. His head really was aching, and he was sprawling in a chair with his wrists tied to the arm-rests. He was in the middle of a huge, dimly lit hall. Dark, gloomy tapestries hung on the wall; a wide stone staircase curved away to his left and vanished in the shadows. Facing him was a cavernous fireplace with a stone hood above on which was embossed a coat of arms within a shield. Ancient pikes and swords were attached to the walls on each side, and from the darkness above there hung an enormous chandelier.

What light there was came from three candles, a mere circle of yellow light in that vast space, and Richard heard a voice, hoarse and rough, to his right, but his head ached when he turned to look.

'He's conscious, *monsieur*,' the voice said.

Two men were looking at Richard. One, presumably the man who had just spoken, was broad-shouldered, squat and immensely powerful in build, dressed in a dark coat and black breeches.

The other was a complete contrast, much younger, and of Richard's own age, richly dressed in a yellow satin coat. His cravat was a master-piece, as Richard's critical eye told him, and beautiful lace frothed at each sleeve of the magnificent coat.

'Keep an eye on him, Paul,' the young man said. 'Have you seen him before?'

'He's not from these parts, *monsieur*. I found all this in his pockets, and this was round his waist.'

The two heads bent down over a small table, and Richard blinked and tried to focus his eyes, but he still felt dizzy and sick.

'Pistols,' the young voice was saying. 'Good ones, too.' A pause. 'This is odd, Paul. These were made in London! What's in that belt?'

The hoarse voice rose in surprise. 'Gold, *monsieur!*' There was a jingle of coins as the sovereigns fell on to the table.

'Let me see, Paul.' Another pause. 'Look here, Paul! These are English sovereigns! There must be nearly a hundred here!' The young man turned and stepped in front of Richard. 'English pistols and English money! And English clothes, too!' He held up a candle and bent down to look at Richard, his sharply featured face alive with curiosity.

'Who are you?' he asked sharply. 'And where are you from?'

Richard licked his dry lips. 'I'm Richard Carey,' he said, 'and I think you must be Armand d'Assailly.'

'What! Carey! Cousin Richard!' Armand snatched at the cord around Richard's wrist. 'Quick, Paul, untie him! Your head, Cousin Richard? I hope Paul didn't hit too hard. What a welcome to Vernaye! Come with me! We must find Mama immediately!'

Excitable young fellow, Richard thought, as he stood up and put a hand to his head. There was a lovely bruise coming up over one ear, and he winced as his fingers touched it. Armand was dragging him across the hall, down a corridor, talking volubly in rapid French, but Richard was too tired and dazed to understand what he was saying.

A door was opened, and Richard found himself being pushed into a brightly lit salon with panelled walls and a painted ceiling. His feet shuffled over a thick carpet, and he blinked at the blaze of lights from the candles. Armand pushed him towards a chair, and he subsided into it gratefully, both hands to his head.

'Armand!' demanded an imperious voice. 'Have you taken leave of your senses? Must you bring every gutter-crawler into my salon?'

Armand laughed. 'Drink this!' he said, and he pushed a heavy goblet into Richard's hand.

Richard took a sip. Brandy, and good brandy, too. He drank, and coughed, and drank again, and the pattern of the carpet between his feet ceased to whirl and heave like the deck of Ianto's sloop.

He raised his head. From the other side of the room a formidable-looking lady was inspecting him with the greatest disgust. She was sitting bolt upright on a wide settee, her back as straight as a musket barrel, trained, no doubt, as Richard decided with an inward grin, on the stools of Versailles. Her clothes, accustomed as he was to the simpler fashions now prevailing in London, were those of another age, for the Marquise de Vernaye was dressed that night as if she were about to attend a ball at Versailles.

Her gown was blue, supported by wide hoops – so wide, indeed, that Richard could understand why she was sitting on a settee, for no ordinary chair would have fitted her. The gown was slit open in front to display a pleated petticoat of a lighter blue. Her hair, assisted by a wig, was piled up carefully to an astonishing height, and crowned with ostrich plumes. In one hand she was holding a little fan, beautifully painted, which she was flicking slowly to and fro so that the lace ruffles at her wrists fluttered gracefully.

'Mama, this is Richard Carey,' Armand said.

Her dark eyes opened; very sharp eyes, Richard noticed, and they were inspecting him closely.

'Nonsense, Armand! This is some common housebreaker that Paul fortunately saw before he could rob me of my jewels. Or perhaps he is one of those unspeakable agitators from Paris.'

Richard stood up a trifle shakily. Brandy on an empty stomach, together with his spinning head and tired legs, made him feel that he would fall flat at any moment. But he bowed as best he could.

'I assure you that I am Richard Carey, Tante Amélie,' he said. 'I have a letter for you from my father,' and he pulled out a creased letter from his breast pocket.

The Marquise took it gingerly, glanced at the writing on the outside, peered at the seal, looked up with sudden interest at Richard and, breaking the seal, began to read. The severity of her face gave way to a smile, a surprisingly charming smile in such a strong face.

'You are indeed Richard,' she said. 'You were an awkward boy when I saw you last. Very awkward,' she added severely. 'Now you have the look of your father about you. No, perhaps your grandfather. He was indeed a grand *seigneur*, Richard. I remember one night at Versailles when he . . .'

'Mama,' Armand broke in, 'I expect Richard is starving, and he looks very tired.'

'Then order him some food, Armand,' the Marquise said calmly. 'Yes, it was the night of a Court Ball in honour of the new Spanish Ambassador, and your grandfather . . .'

'Mama!'

'Yes, Armand, what is it now?'

'Please, Mama, Richard hasn't come to talk about Versailles.'

The Marquise was unmoved by the rebuke, nor did she treat the remark as an impertinence, somewhat to Richard's surprise. Perhaps her family found it necessary to cut short her reminiscences, for it was clear that she lived in the past.

'We all know why Richard has come,' she said. 'But, my dear Armand,

there is a certain decorum to be observed, even in these days of revolution. The art of polite conversation . . .'

'Then you should present Richard to Louise,' Armand said.

'Louise!' The Marquise turned her head slowly, as indeed she would have to, Richard thought, crowned as she was with that colossal mountain of hair and ostrich plumes.

Richard turned, too, for a girl had just come into the room. This must be the untidy, silent child he could remember vaguely, and he bowed politely over her hand, wondering how quickly Armand's servant could bring some food for him. He had not been so hungry for years.

He straightened his long back and smiled down courteously. 'Cousin Louise,' he said. His grip on her hand tightened, and the smile left his face. 'Er . . . er . . . Cousin Louise, it . . . it is a great pleasure to meet you again,' he stammered, and he found that he was still holding her hand.

For the uninteresting little girl was now an extremely beautiful one, with an alert and intelligent expression that he had so often told his mother was entirely lacking from the faces of the young ladies she invited to Berkeley Square and Llanstephan Hall.

Louise flushed, and Richard hastily released her hand. He moved back and saw that the dark eyes of the Marquise were positively snapping with delight. Trust her not to miss his embarrassment, Richard thought. So there was something in this family arrangement, after all. And that was why his mother had never raised any objections to his visit to France; he had been surprised at that, and now he grinned. Well, he didn't mind, either.

At that moment, and much to his relief, a servant brought in a tray, and pulled up a small table under Armand's directions.

'If you will excuse me, Tante Amélie,' Richard said, but he would have started to eat whatever this formidable lady might have said. There was an omelette on the tray, and he could smell the lovely fragrance of freshly made coffee.

'By all means, my dear Richard,' the Marquise said. 'But you must tell us exactly how you came to arrive in this melodramatic fashion.'

Between mouthfuls Richard told his story. 'Incidentally, Tante,' he said, 'Uncle Rupert sends you his regards.'

The Marquise laughed delightedly. 'Dear Rupert,' she said. 'I have a suspicion that it was he who planned all this.' She chuckled as Richard nodded. His mouth was too full to answer. 'I might have known,' she added. 'He has a flair for violence and dramatics. I remember that when he was last at Versailles, your Uncle Quentin had the greatest difficulty in preventing him from fighting at least two duels. Not that there was any difficulty with his opponents. They were terrified, and with good reason.' The fan fluttered rapidly as she laughed again.

Armand broke in again before his mother could begin another series of stories about Versailles.

'Mama, we must talk about the arrangements for sailing to England,' he said. 'What has Uncle Rupert planned, Richard?'

'The sloop will be off the beach for the next three nights.'

'Tomorrow night, then,' Armand said decisively, and Richard looked at his distant cousin with approval. Another intelligent person who knew his mind.

'Mama, Louise, will you have everything packed that you want to take with you? It can't be much, you know,' and he looked at Richard, who nodded his instant agreement. His brain reeled at the thought of how much the Marquise would consider necessary. Poor Ianto would have to send a procession of boats to the beach.

But Richard's secret amusement was interrupted by an explosion from the Marquise. For five minutes she informed everyone in the room that she had no intention of running away from France; she saw not the slightest reason why she should do so.

Armand sighed. He had obviously heard all this before. 'You are no longer safe in France, Mama,' he said. 'They have already arrested Father.'

The fan waved this argument to oblivion. Paris was one place, the Marquise pointed out, and Normandy another. Backwards and forwards went the battle, and Richard, who had finished his meal, leant back and listened to the rapid exchanges in excitable French, the waving fan, the expressive hands and shoulders. He caught a glance from Louise, and grinned at her; she flushed and dropped her eyes again.

'One of the coaches will be ready at eleven tomorrow night,' Armand said at last. 'Make certain you have your jewels, Mama. The rest you must leave.'

'Must we leave like paupers?' his mother demanded.

'We shall be nothing of the kind,' Armand said. 'Thanks to Richard's father and his forethought, we transferred ample funds three years ago. And you will have the choice of either Llanstephan or Horton in which to live. Will you be spending the summer in Wales, Richard?'

Richard was to have travelled to the Mediterranean with Rupert. But he glanced briefly at Louise, and nodded his head emphatically. 'I had planned to be at Llanstephan,' he said promptly.

The Marquise shrugged her shoulders to admit defeat, and then announced that she and Louise were going to bed. Armand closed the door behind them and came back to sit by Richard.

He smiled at his cousin. 'Mama refuses to admit that anything has happened in France since 1789,' he said.

Richard lounged sleepily in his chair, his long legs stretched out now that the Marquise had left. He could not imagine anyone sprawling untidily in a chair while that straight-backed and formidable lady was about.

'*Is* there much danger for you here, Armand?' he asked.

'It's difficult to say. But Papa has always been a good landlord, and we have spent much of our time here, you see. We are well liked, I think. But it would be foolish to run the risk. Even if the local people did nothing, orders might come from Paris.'

Richard yawned enormously, and Armand sprang to his feet. 'I am so sorry, Richard,' he said. 'You must be exhausted. I will show you to your room.'

He took two candles from the mantelpiece, and led Richard across the great, bare hall, and up the main staircase, along a wide corridor, and then he flung open the door of a room where candles were already alight.

'Good,' he said, 'I told Gavril to have everything ready for you. We have sent most of the servants away, you see. I hope this will be satisfactory, Richard. This is not the way we should have liked to entertain you on your first visit to Vernaye.'

Richard looked indifferently around the large bedroom, for he was interested only in the four-poster bed, the white sheets and the inviting pile of soft pillows.

'I shall be very comfortable, Armand,' he said, and he started to take off his coat. Five minutes later he was sprawling on the bed, reaching for the last candle to blow it out.

When Richard awoke he lay for a moment in the warm, stuffy darkness and wondered where he was. Then he stretched luxuriously; his head was sore to touch, but his tiredness had vanished, and he felt once more that he could enjoy this affair. The most difficult part, after all, was now over. He had found the Assailly family, and Ianto Price would do the rest.

He groped his way to the tall curtains and pulled them back. Bright morning sunlight streamed into the room, and with an effort Richard opened the window. Below was the formal garden he had seen the previous night. Beyond and as far as he could see were trees, a dark green mass that apparently surrounded the château on every side. He could hear doves cooing softly, but otherwise there was complete silence: the great château seemed as remote and unreal, as completely divorced from the noisy world as it had seemed to him in the moonlight a few hours before.

He pulled a bell-rope by the door, and a footman came almost immediately. He was respectful and polite, so presumably not everyone in the Normandy countryside was intent on burning châteaux and arresting aristocrats. He brought hot water and a selection of clothes, but they were all far too small for Richard. The Assailly family, clearly, did not approach their Welsh cousins in size.

Richard dressed reluctantly in the old clothes which he had worn when he left the sloop, and regarded himself with disgust in the mirror. He looked like one of his father's gamekeepers, he thought. What would Louise think when she saw him? What he would have given for his new brown coat and white breeches, and a pair of his gleaming Hessian boots! He tugged irritably at the silk scarf, but however he arranged it, it still looked an untidy mess compared to the neat cravat that he usually wore. He cursed Rupert and his ideas of travelling light, and went down the great stone staircase into the hall below.

There was no one to be seen, and he had no idea where to find the dining-room. The French, he remembered gloomily, did not believe in large breakfasts, and he was extremely hungry. He thought with longing of ham, eggs, a round of cold beef, the long sideboard at Llanstephan with its choice of dishes, and sighed.

The great doors of the château were open, and he strolled out on to a wide sweep of gravel outside. Everything at Vernaye appeared to be on a vast scale, he thought, and then he saw a figure in green crossing one of the lawns below the terrace. His pace quickened, and he almost trotted down the steps.

'Good morning, Cousin Louise,' he said.

Louise had not heard him, and as she turned she flushed with confusion and dropped her eyes.

Richard hesitated and shuffled his feet, and half smiled, the self-confident young man of fashion who was never at a loss for the right word.

'I say, Louise, I'm starving,' he said.

'Haven't you had any breakfast, Richard?' she said, and they both laughed as the slight feeling of restraint vanished. 'I'll show you the dining-room.'

Richard had a better breakfast than he had expected, and he finished an enormous quantity of fresh rolls, still warm from the oven, honey and butter, and several cups of coffee that Louise poured for him.

'Has Armand told you, Richard?' she asked, when he had finally pushed away his plate.

'I haven't seen him this morning,' he said. 'What should he tell me?'

'He is not coming with us.'

'Not coming! To Wales, you mean?' He stared at Louise. 'But what's he going to do, then?'

'He's determined to go to Paris. Papa is there, you see.'

'I know,' Richard said. 'But there's nothing Armand can do to help Uncle Quentin, is there?'

Louise's shoulders lifted doubtfully. 'Perhaps not. But Armand is very obstinate, Richard. He says that he can't possibly run away and leave Papa.'

Richard rubbed his chin uncomfortably. This business had seemed somewhat unreal in England, for he barely knew these French cousins of his. But now he was far more closely involved, too closely for his peace of mind. He felt an uneasy twinge; he was running away to England, too. He tried to push the thought away; after all, he had been given a definite task, and he must carry it out.

'Does Tante Amélie know?' he asked.

'Armand is going to tell her at the last moment. She would never leave Vernaye if she thought Armand was staying in France.'

'No, I suppose not,' Richard said, but at that moment Armand came into the room and began to discuss the arrangements for going down to the coast that night. Then he and Louise took Richard on a tour of the château.

The main state-rooms were not in use, and the furniture was covered with dust-sheets, and the windows curtained. But Richard saw enough to realize that Vernaye was probably twice the size of Llanstephan Hall. He was not envious. Magnificent as was Vernaye, its scale was too large for him, its atmosphere too stiff and formal. His own home was large, of course, and possessed many fine rooms; the Great Chamber and the Long Gallery were considered to be among the finest examples of Elizabethan architecture and design in the country, but the house still retained an air of comfort and homeliness which was lacking at Vernaye.

They ate a late dinner, and the Marquise was dissuaded with some difficulty from dressing formally; never, she said, had she dined in her travelling clothes, but she did so that evening. The food and cooking were as fine as Richard had ever experienced, and so, too, were the wines. But they ate in silence for the most part, and it was with a sense of relief that Richard went up to his room to collect his few belongings. He strapped on his sword-belt, checked both pistols to see that they were loaded and primed, and went down to the entrance hall.

All the candles had been lighted, as if for some great entertainment in the château, and all the servants who had remained with the family were drawn up facing the doors. Many of them were in tears, and all showed a genuine and touching distress. Louise broke down completely, and Armand was deeply moved. As for the Marquise, she had been brought up in the rigid school of Versailles, where any display of emotion was kept under firm control. She stood in silence as each servant came forward to curtsey to her, and her strong face never quivered or showed any feeling beyond that of a great lady greeting her servants. But when the last muttered farewell had been made, she marched resolutely past Richard and through the double doors, and only then did he see the tears that were streaming down her cheeks.

Outside, a damp ground-mist had drifted over the terrace and the gardens. The blazing lights from the hall threw a broad yellow gleam out on to the huge gravel forecourt and the coach and four horses standing there. As Richard opened the door for the Marquise he felt once more the unreality of all this. For over their heads loomed the façade of the château, a greyish blur in the mist, and all around was the circle of trees and that eerie atmosphere of remoteness that seemed to engulf the whole place.

Three horses were led up for Armand, Richard and the gigantic man-servant, Paul, who had nearly cracked Richard's skull the previous night. A sharp word of command from Armand, and the heavy coach lurched forward. The doors of the château clanged behind them with a sound of utter finality, and Richard saw Armand turn in his saddle and look back before they swung round a corner in the drive. Then the clinging mist closed round them, and they were in a small world of two yellow lights from the lanterns of the coach, and the lines of trees on either side, their topmost branches rising above the grey mist.

Richard followed Armand; they were not taking the lane he had used, he noticed, but he could tell that they were dropping gradually towards the coast, and to his great relief the mist shredded away. Ianto would never see the signal lantern unless the night was fairly clear.

Then they were riding along a level road, and on the right were the sand dunes, and Richard could hear the sea. Armand reined in, and the coach creaked to a halt.

'I'll go down with Paul and signal,' Richard said.

Armand nodded, and Paul lifted one of the oil lanterns from the clip in front of the coach. They found a gap in the dunes and rode slowly over the sand until Richard stopped by the edge of the water. The night was perfect for their purpose, for the full moon was up now, and the whole beach was clearly revealed.

'Hold up the lantern, Paul,' Richard said. 'Cover it with your hat. Three times, pause, and then once again.'

He stared out to sea over the gently moving water, black and oily in the moonlight, wondering if he could pick out the shape of the sloop. But he could see nothing.

'Again, Paul,' Richard said.

He sat there fighting down his rising fears. He did not know Ianto Price well; was the smuggler still lying off the coast? Could he find his way back without a mistake to the same beach? Had he lost his nerve, and sailed back to Wales?

'Nothing, *monsieur*,' Paul said.

'Try again,' Richard said. He hoped his voice betrayed none of his thoughts. He tried to remember that Rupert had picked Price for this affair. He could not believe that Rupert would have chosen the wrong man.

Armand drew up alongside. 'They are bringing Mama and Louise down now,' he said. 'Any signal, Richard?'

'Nothing yet. One lantern on the beach is a poor light,' he said.

'They're bringing the other lamp from the coach,' Armand said, and at that moment one of the coachmen trotted up and joined Paul in the signalling. The Marquise and Louise were standing miserably on the sand, peering out over the unfriendly expanse of water.

'Nothing!' Armand said. 'This is no use, Richard. We shall . . .'

'There!' Louise cried, and she pointed out to sea. 'I'm sure I saw a flash. Yes, there, Armand!'

Silence fell on the group, broken by a shout of delight from Armand. Richard could see the light now, a series of sharp flashes, and he thought, too, he could distinguish the darker bulk of the sloop. He sighed, and his fist that had been clenching the reins convulsively, relaxed its grip.

'Quiet!' Armand hissed. 'I heard a boat!'

Richard heard the thump and rattle of oars in the rowlocks, and there, suddenly, was the shape of a rowing boat coming towards them, and behind it another one.

Richard twitched his reins and rode forward into the water.

'Ianto!' he shouted.

'Mr Carey!' came back the answering hail. There was no mistaking that Welsh voice with the rise in the intonation towards the end of the name, and Richard laughed aloud. Those minutes of waiting had been long and frightening. Old Rupert was right again when he had warned Richard that waiting was the worst part of any action.

The two boats were run up on to the sand, and the tall figure of Ianto splashed his way towards Richard.

'There's punctual you are, Mr Carey,' he said.

Richard laughed a trifle shakily. 'I'm glad to see you, Ianto.'

'*Duw*, man, whyeffer not?' Ianto said. 'This is kid's play, Mr Carey. Now, the ladies first, Sir Rupert said. And the baggage in the other boat.'

Before she could protest, the Marquise was whirled off her feet by Ianto, carried through the shallow water, and dumped in one of the boats. Richard grinned. She had said nothing, but her thoughts must have been searing. There was something to be said for the training of the old school.

The cases were quickly thrown into the other boat, and both pulled away and out of sight. Armand edged his horse towards Richard.

'Did Louise tell you, Richard?' he said. 'I'm not coming.'

'Yes, she did. But you can't do anything on your own, Armand. Are you really determined to go to Paris?'

'Quite determined.' There was no mistaking the complete finality of his reply.

Richard sat there uneasily. In five minutes he would be safely on board the sloop. Within a few days he would be sitting in the Great Chamber of Llanstephan, or walking with Louise in the garden that overlooked the sea. And Armand would be making his way towards Paris and all the dangers that awaited him there, intent on his hopeless task, with the prospect that he would almost certainly join his father in prison, and with him take the slow journey through the streets to the guillotine.

From the sand dunes behind came a loud shout and the crack of a pistol. Richard turned his head, and from his open mouth there came a gasp of sheer fright. Three horsemen had burst into view, quite clearly to be seen in the moonlight, and were galloping down the beach towards them. Fifty yards or so to the right was another group of riders, and they, too, were moving towards the water.

7

Monsieur Gribeauval

Richard heard shouts, and could distinguish some of the words.

'Halt! In the name of the Republic! Halt!'

He was quite unable to move. He sat there in his saddle and stared. He was frightened, horrified, and for the first time in his life he knew what sheer terror meant, that freezing of the muscles, the nauseating sense of emptiness in his stomach.

He thought he stayed like that for a minute at least. But it was probably a second only before his hand dived into the pocket of his coat and pulled out a pistol. Even in that moment of panic he wondered if Rupert's screw-barrel pistol would indeed be so accurate. Fifty yards, he had said. So wait, he thought; distance was deceptive in this light, and he had two shots only, for there would be no time to reload.

Up came his hand, the heavy pistol very steady in his grasp, until the long barrel was level and aiming at the centre horseman in the group of three as they thundered over the wet sand.

Richard squeezed the trigger. A blinding flash in front of his eyes, a loud, flat report, and a riderless horse swerved and reared to the right.

'Fire, Paul, fire!' Armand was shrieking.

Richard stuffed the empty pistol back into his pocket, and was groping for the second one. He heard a bang from the left, saw the flash of Armand's pistol, and from behind him Paul suddenly fired, and a second rider threw up an arm and slid sideways from the saddle.

Richard was up to the aim again, squinted briefly along the black line of the barrel, and fired. The pistol jerked in his hand, and he blinked in the sudden flash. He had never fired pistols at night before, and for a moment his eyes were half blinded. But he saw the third rider bend down, heard his shout, and watched him topple to the sand.

'*A gauche! A gauche!*' Armand was yelling, and he set off along the beach.

The second group of riders was swinging down from the dunes, and spreading out in a line. But Richard did not hesitate this time. He kicked his spurs into his unfortunate horse's flanks, pulled its head round with a jerk on the reins, and flew along the beach, ducking his head and cursing as the sand and water flew up from Armand's horse.

Armand was veering round gradually towards the line of the dunes. Richard glanced over his shoulder. Paul's ponderous figure was just behind and to the left; the pursuers were a hundred yards away at least.

He could see a wide gap in the dunes, and Armand pulled his horse round abruptly to the right again, and they all three headed for the same spot. Then they had left the soft sand, and were clattering along the lane that ran parallel with the sea.

'*A droit!*' Armand shouted. He set his horse at the low hedge, soared up in the air and vanished on the other side.

'Hope you can jump,' Richard muttered to his horse. 'Now!' and his horse lifted beneath him. 'Wonder what's on the other side.'

But the ground was soft, though Richard was jolted badly, for it was difficult to see clearly enough in the moonlight, and then his horse was galloping over a flat piece of heathland, climbing a slight slope and heading for a welcome line of trees about a hundred yards ahead.

They shot through the first few trees, and Armand swerved again, and to the left, and there was a narrow avenue through the woods, winding now and then, but leading steadily inland. They were in the mist again, and the visibility was so poor that Richard was nearly swept out of his saddle by overhanging branches. But he did not mind that; the thicker the mist, the safer they would be from pursuit.

At last Armand reined in and Richard drew up alongside. Armand was sitting limply in the saddle, with one hand to his shoulder.

'What's the matter?' Richard asked sharply.

'Hit in the shoulder,' Armand muttered.

Paul and Richard dismounted and helped Armand down. Quickly and efficiently Paul produced a white scarf and began to bandage the wound, while Richard held the horses.

The exhilaration of the swift and violent action on the beach, the wild ride through the woods had left him, though it had indeed been exhilarating, he realized. He felt chilled now, standing there in the clinging mist with the trees dripping overhead, and the moisture running down his coat. But the discomfort was the least of his worries. He was stranded in France now; the retreat to the sloop was cut off; he had no friends to go to, nowhere to spend the night. Ahead lay an unfriendly countryside, and all the unknown dangers and complete uncertainty of the immediate future.

There was little left now of the self-confident young man who had driven his curricle from London to Wales a week ago. Everything that had made his comfortable existence possible had vanished. No well-found and luxurious inn with bowing servants lay round the corner of the road; his money, the sovereigns in his belt, were probably useless. He was indeed standing on his own feet at last, and in that blinding moment of truth he knew now what Rupert had meant.

'That was wonderful shooting, Richard,' Armand said. 'Two shots at fifty yards, and both men down.'

'Yes, they're good pistols,' Richard said. 'But I haven't reloaded. Rupert told me I must always reload as soon as I get the chance.'

With shaking hands he fumbled with powder and bullets and the wrench for unscrewing the barrels. But it was done at last, and as he pushed the pistols back into the holsters on each side of his saddle, he smiled a little ruefully. For he had learnt something else, and he was wishing he had known it before. But it was odd how frequently he thought of Rupert now. All that last-minute advice to which he had listened with half-concealed impatience was so much to the point. Rupert had prepared him for most emergencies, and he wished that the wiry little man was standing by his side now. Because Rupert would have known exactly what to do next; his brisk voice would have said just the right things to cheer them up. His uncle, Richard realized with shame at his own blindness, was a remarkable man; he had always liked him, but he knew now that he admired him, too.

'How is it with you, Armand?' he asked, now that the three were once more remounted.

'The bullet went right through my arm,' Armand said. 'My head's swimming. I must have lost a good deal of blood.'

Richard could see, even in that light, that Armand was liable to fall out of his saddle at any moment. The next move must come from him; Paul was stolid and reliable, but he was accustomed to obeying orders, not making plans, and Armand was in no condition to lead them much farther.

'We can't go back to Vernaye,' Richard said slowly. 'I don't know who those men were on the beach, or how they got there. But they seemed to know all about us.'

'They may have seen the coach by chance,' Armand said. 'How could they have known we would be on the beach at that hour?'

'I can't understand that either,' Richard said. 'But they arrived just a little too promptly for my liking. Anyway, we've got to find shelter and have that shoulder of yours seen to. Look, Armand, we must still be on Vernaye land. What about your tenants? Is there a farm we can go to?'

'Several,' Armand said. 'But no one would be prepared to take the risk of hiding me if they knew that Government agents were after me.'

Richard shrugged his shoulders gloomily. He could think of no solution; if Armand had not been wounded, then they could have hidden in the woods for the night, and tried to make some sort of contact with Ianto Price the next evening. But he had an uneasy suspicion that the coast would be watched.

'Paul!' Armand said suddenly. 'How far are we from Colombey-sur-Thaon? Ten miles?'

'Closer than that, *monsieur*.'

'Right! Then we'll try old Gribeauval.'

'Who's he?' Richard asked hopefully.

'My father's estate agent and bailiff.'

'But can you trust him?'

'I'm sure of it,' Armand said confidently. 'He'd risk his life for my family.'

'That's just what he will be doing,' Richard said. 'We've shot three men. Government agents probably. Anyone who shelters us now will be in the same boat.'

'Gribeauval would give his head for Father,' Armand said. 'Paul, you know the way. Take the lead.'

They rode through the mist for a couple of hours, with Paul in front, and Richard riding by Armand's side, watching him anxiously, and wondering how much longer his cousin would last before he fainted. They seemed to be travelling away from the coast, and Paul never hesitated, despite the darkness and the lack of signposts in the deserted country lanes they followed, still with tall banks on either side.

Then they trotted through a village of one street, with white cottages and shuttered windows, and a church with a squat tower, past which Paul led them, turning down the lane beyond and through a gate to a house that stood back from the road.

It was a low, two-storeyed building of medium size, with a mansard roof and whitewashed walls. All the windows were shuttered, and no lights could be seen, though that was hardly surprising at that time of night, Richard thought hopefully.

Paul dismounted and beat a tattoo with the little knocker on the door. Armand drooped in his saddle, and Richard held him up. Armand, it was clear, had reached the end of his strength.

Three times Paul knocked, waiting patiently, apparently unmoved by their desperate position, and when at last a shutter creaked above their heads, he said nothing but merely looked up in silence, as if he had no doubts or fears. Richard could distinguish a white blob of a face peering down at them.

'Who is that?' a deep voice asked, a remarkably composed voice, too, for a man awakened in the middle of the night, and in a countryside in turmoil.

'It is I, Armand d'Assailly,' Armand said faintly.

'Monsieur le Vicomte!' There was a shade of great surprise in the deep voice. 'Wait! I will be down immediately.'

Richard dismounted, and Armand heeled over into his arms. Paul took one arm, and they half carried him to the door. Bolts rattled inside, a chain clanked, and the door swung open to reveal a narrow hall and a short figure in a coat flung over a nightgown, one arm holding a candlestick.

'I'll stable the horses,' Paul said, and he disappeared.

'In here, *monsieur*,' the old man said, and he held open a door on the left.

Richard hauled Armand's limp figure into the room and lowered him on to a settee. Armand had fainted, and Richard bent over him anxiously, but a firm hand pushed him to one side.

'Let me see, *monsieur*,' the deep, calm voice said. 'Yes, I will fetch warm water and bandages.'

He put down the candle and left the room. Richard heard him speak in the hall. 'Ah, it is you, Paul Legendre. We want hot water and bandages. And something hot to drink. You know where things are in the kitchen?'

Richard looked down helplessly at Armand's sprawling figure. But some of his worry had gone; this old man, Gribeauval presumably, seemed to have accepted the position with surprising calmness.

Paul and Gribeauval returned with armfuls of white cloths, basins and steaming water, and Richard sat down on a chair; there was nothing he could do to help these two, and he was glad of the chance to rest. Odd how tired he felt, he thought; probably the reaction after the swift action of the last few hours. He wondered what Ianto Price was doing. He would almost certainly try again the next night, but he would probably approach the beach with some caution. Anyway, there was not the slightest chance of finding Richard there. Armand would not be able to move for a week. Richard did not quite know what he was going to do, but of one thing he was certain. He was not going to desert Armand now.

'A bad flesh wound,' Gribeauval said. 'Rest and sleep will cure him. Now, Legendre, let us make use of your great strength and carry the Vicomte upstairs.' He turned to Richard. 'If you will wait here, *monsieur*, I will bring you a hot drink and some food.'

Richard stretched out his legs and listened to the stumbling footsteps on the stairs. He looked round the small room, furnished more as an office than a salon, with a large desk covered with neat stacks of documents in one corner.

The door opened and Gribeauval came in, with Paul behind him carrying a tray. Richard drank the hot coffee gratefully, and munched greedily at the bread and cheese, while the old man sat down opposite and watched him in silence. Richard inspected him warily, for their lives depended upon this old man, and old indeed he was – in his late seventies, Richard thought – with wispy white hair, a huge brow over a pair of deep-set eyes, a firm chin and mouth, and an air of unshakeable composure.

'I do not know your face, *monsieur*,' he said.

'My name is Carey,' Richard said.

'Carey.' The faded eyes were still shrewd enough. 'There is an English family of that name. They are connections of the Marquis. But why are you in France, Monsieur Carey?'

Richard told his story. Gribeauval was a good listener; he nodded his head occasionally, but he made no comment until Richard had finished.

'Well, you will be safe enough here for the time being,' Gribeauval said. 'I think some sleep would do you good, too, Monsieur Carey. I will show you a bedroom. This is a large house for just myself and my old house-keeper, so we have several empty rooms.'

He lighted a candle for Richard and led him up the narrow stairs to a small and plainly furnished room. He bade Richard a polite goodnight and left him. Richard dragged off his damp coat and trousers, and rolled on to the bed. It was as hard as a board after the comfortable bed in which he had slept at the château, but he was too tired to worry, and a bed of any kind was more than he had hoped for that night.

Armand was still asleep, but apparently there was nothing to worry about, Paul told Richard the next morning. Richard ate his breakfast with Gribeauval, a small, trim figure in a black coat and knee-breeches; it was a good breakfast in the French fashion, and Richard enjoyed the fresh rolls and the thick farm butter, yellow and salty like the Carmarthenshire butter they made at Llanstephan.

In the morning light he took another long look at Gribeauval and was reassured by what he saw; the old man still gave him that comforting impression of trustworthiness and composure, and he seemed a very intelligent old gentleman, too, with his ascetic face, the white, wrinkled skin stretched tightly over the strong chin and beaky nose.

'When do you think the Vicomte will be able to travel?' Richard asked.

'Not for two weeks at least, Monsieur Carey. He has lost a great deal of blood, and he is very weak.' Gribeauval took off the spectacles that were perched on his bony nose, and polished them with a white handkerchief. 'You will be quite safe here, Monsieur Carey.'

'I daresay,' Richard said. 'But you are taking a considerable risk, Monsieur Gribeauval. We . . .'

'I am perfectly aware of the danger,' Gribeauval said calmly. 'I expect you are wondering if you are wise to trust me, eh?' and he smiled as he saw the embarrassed expression on Richard's face. 'Why not?' he asked. 'You know nothing of me, do you?'

'Er . . . no, I don't,' Richard said.

'Well, I will tell you something about myself, and then you can decide if you still wish to remain here.' He held up the spectacles to the light, and put them back on his nose. 'I was a lawyer in Paris,' he said. 'I dealt with the affairs of the Assailly family among others. I have a son, *monsieur*. He was young and very impetuous, and like many of his generation he read Rousseau and Voltaire. Are you familiar with their works, *monsieur?*'

Richard nodded. As part of his teaching in French, he had read some of Voltaire's books, and he had dipped into Rousseau's *Social Contract*.

'Heady stuff, *monsieur*, is it not? Too heady for my son. He was arrested for helping to publish a pamphlet attacking the King and his ministers. Deservedly so, I suppose. The pamphlet was a very bitter one.'

'What happened to him?'

'He should have gone to the galleys. That would have been a slow and painful death, *monsieur*. But the Marquis de Vernaye came to our help. So my son is still alive. He is not so impetuous now. He is living the placid life of a lawyer in Rennes.'

He started to polish his spectacles again.

'But that is not all my family owes to the Marquis. My wife fell ill. The Marquis sent for the greatest doctors in Paris. He would not let me pay a sou, *monsieur*, and the bills were enormous. My wife is dead now, but thanks to the Marquis we enjoyed another fifteen years together.' The old man looked at Richard and smiled. 'So you see, Monsieur Carey, you are quite safe in my house.'

'I think we are very lucky,' Richard said. 'And I am sorry I ever doubted you, Monsieur Gribeauval.'

The old lawyer shook his head. 'I am very puzzled by those horsemen on the beach at Graye-sur-Mer,' he said.

'So am I. I don't like the sound of it at all,' Richard said.

'You may be right, *monsieur*. But there's nothing we can do. So you must make the most of what my small house offers for the next week or so. I have a good selection of books, and there is a walled garden in which you can sit. I should not go into the village. Your French is excellent, *monsieur*, but I should take no risks.'

Three slow and restful days passed. Armand was still in bed, but the wound was healing, and some of the colour had returned to his face. Richard spent most of his time in the walled garden, and usually lay under the trees reading. What they were going to do when Armand recovered he did not know. At least Armand knew; he was still determined to go to Paris, and Richard wished he could make up his mind so easily.

That third afternoon was warm and sultry, and Richard had dropped his book and was dozing, his head and back propped against the trunk of a tree.

'Ah, Monsieur Carey,' a voice said. 'I have found you at last!'

Richard opened his eyes and scrambled to his feet. 'De Marillac!' he exclaimed. 'But I thought you were in London. Good heavens, has old Rupert sent you over, too?' He laughed with delight and relief.

De Marillac shook his head and stepped back a pace. His right hand which he was holding behind his back came into view. Richard found himself staring at the dark muzzle of a small pistol, and it was pointed unwaveringly at his heart.

8

The Duel in the Garden

'What the devil!' Richard said incredulously. He saw de Marillac's finger pull back the cocking-piece with a click, and he looked up at the man's dark face and the hard eyes that were gleaming now with malicious amusement. But even in that moment of utter shock Richard's brain was working, a sure sign that he was learning quickly in this world of action into which he had been plunged.

'Oh, now I see,' he said slowly. 'You were one of those men at Graye-sur-Mer.'

'I was. My visit to London was extremely useful.' De Marillac's white teeth showed briefly in a smile. He was obviously enjoying his sudden and dramatic appearance in the garden. Rather like a cat teasing a mouse,

Richard thought, trying to ignore that dreadful feeling of emptiness that had swept over him, and which he now knew was fear.

'And the Vicomte d'Assailly?' de Marillac asked. 'I think one of my men hit him?'

'Wounded,' Richard said. 'In the shoulder. So you're in the pay of the new Republic,' he added, and he made no attempt to hide the contempt in his voice.

De Marillac flushed. 'I must live somehow,' he said, 'and the old regime did little enough for me. No, no, Monsieur Carey. Don't move! I could hardly miss at this range.'

Richard shrugged his shoulders. There was nothing he could do, except play for time, perhaps, in the faint hope that Paul might suddenly appear from the house. But Paul had gone into the village an hour ago. Could he make de Marillac lose his temper, and so give him a chance to grab that pistol?

'You were acting as a spy in London, then,' he said, 'while you were accepting our hospitality?'

De Marillac stiffened, and his glance at Richard was venomous. 'And what are you doing in France, Monsieur Carey?' he asked. 'Spying, too? Skulking around the countryside, aiding the enemies of the Republic, shooting Government agents? You killed two men that night, do you know? No, you are working for your Government, and I am working for mine.'

'I'm not working for any Government,' Richard said, his eyes on the pistol. But the infernal thing had not shifted an inch. 'Even if I were, there would still be a difference of motives, you know. You are doing it for money, presumably, while I would be . . .'

'For honour, I suppose.' The Frenchman's voice had risen, but he was still watching Richard closely. 'It's easy enough to talk like that, Monsieur Carey, when you have money.'

'Well, if it's money you want,' Richard said, seeing his chance, 'we can pay you well. Help Armand d'Assailly and myself to England, and my father will see that you won't lose. He's a rich man.'

De Marillac eyed Richard reflectively, and for a second or two Richard thought he had won. Then the Frenchman shook his head. 'Too risky,' he said. 'The ports are too closely watched, and not even I could produce passports for you both.'

'What are you going to do, then?'

'Take you both to Paris.'

'But the Vicomte is a sick man,' Richard said. 'You can't move him now.'

'I can find a coach. My men are at Secqueville-en-Bessin, twenty kilometres from here.'

A flicker of hope stirred in Richard's brain. 'Oh, you're by yourself, then?'

De Marillac laughed. 'Quite alone! But don't build on that. I want all the credit for this myself. I can easily find someone here who will see that Armand d'Assailly stays in the house while I take you to Secqueville.'

He moved to one side, and kicked away Richard's sword, which was lying in its scabbard on the grass. He gestured with the pistol towards the farther end of the garden, where there was a door opening on to the road.

'That way, Monsieur Carey.'

Richard sighed. Then, as he stepped forward, his face suddenly lightened, and he shouted, 'Quick, Paul, the pistol, man!'

De Marillac spun round with a curse. But there was no one behind him. The garden was deserted. Richard's long arm reached out for his wrist, twisted fiercely, and as the pistol dropped, his right fist caught de Marillac on the side of the jaw and sent him sprawling on the grass.

But the Frenchman was as quick as a cat. He was up on his feet again, and had whipped out his sword. Richard had half reached down for the pistol, but it was just too far away. Instead he jumped back, snatched up his own sword and pulled it out of the scabbard, and they both stood there for a moment, panting with their sudden efforts.

'Very well, Monsieur Carey,' de Marillac said. 'You can finish your short life here if you wish. It is of no importance to me if you die in this garden or under the guillotine in Paris. Armand d'Assailly is the man I am after.'

There was none of the polite formality of the fencing school as de

Marillac slid forward his right foot on the dry, smooth turf, and extended himself in a murderous lunge for Richard's chest.

Desperately Richard brought his sword across; a loud clink, a harsh clash of steel, and he had pushed the long blade away. De Marillac disengaged with a speed that was ominous, and again the menacing strip of steel leapt towards Richard. He parried clumsily and drew a deep breath of sheer terror. The Frenchman was obviously a very fine swordsman, faster than anyone Richard had ever faced except old Loubet, perhaps, but this was no harmless bout with the foils, it was Richard's first engagement with a naked blade.

De Marillac cut over and lunged again with the same bewildering speed and smoothness. Once more Richard parried, but he had no time to attempt a riposte. He was thankful enough to keep off that frightful swordpoint. A vision of himself impaled like a pig on a skewer flashed through his head; so vivid was the picture that already he could feel the searing pain in his chest as if de Marillac had driven his sword through him.

De Marillac lunged in carte; with the same clumsy haste Richard parried; he saw the other's blade disengage, and then a white-hot skewer, or so it seemed, shot through his arm, and he jumped back with a cry. But there was no hope of shouting '*Touché*' now, to show that he had been hit, and a polite bow from his opponent before they resumed the bout.

Instead de Marillac hissed triumphantly; his face was set and intent, his dark eyes implacable as he stepped forward and lunged again with the same merciless precision and speed.

Two minutes, or much longer – Richard could not tell – passed in a blurred nightmare of endless plunges and frantic parries. His arm was throbbing, and he could feel a warm stickiness inside the sleeve. He might be losing a good deal of blood; his sword arm might weaken fatally at any moment. He could not last much longer, and he had not so much as made a real attack yet.

Only his long training, the daily practice and his great technical skill kept de Marillac's blade away, and even then Richard's defence was a clumsy imitation of his normal fencing. But he suddenly realized that his

opponent was breathing hard, and that his temper was rising; his tremendous exertions and all his skill were still useless against this ponderous Englishman who was holding him off by some miracle.

He paused for a fraction of a second, the first real break in the smooth sequence of his attacks. Richard disengaged and lunged, but slowly and a trifle too late. His blade was swept away with contemptuous ease, but in that moment Richard had slipped into his own rhythm of fencing.

He parried de Marillac's next lunge and cut over with a speed that he had never shown before, and so unexpected was his attack that de Marillac saved himself by a parry while still on the lunge himself. He straightened his back and jumped to one side.

He spat and hissed like an angry cat, and then Richard went for him in a berserk fury, a mixture of fear and desperation and loathing. There was no clumsiness now; his finger-play was that of a master; his disengagements swift and deadly in their speed; and his long reach made each thrust so dangerous that it was de Marillac who was now parrying with a cumbersome haste. His coat sleeve was ripped across by one lunge, and Richard laughed, a bark of triumph and determination. He had forgotten the wound in his arm; he never paused to think that he was fighting a superb swordsman who might run him through if he faltered; his whole mind was filled with the one aim of killing this little rat.

De Marillac had fallen back to keep clear of that long reach, and they were both in the centre of the lawn now, two stabbing, thrusting figures, moving in short, quick steps, breathing hoarsely, their feet stamping on the hard ground, grunting, lunging, their blades clashing in a continual clangour of sound.

The Frenchman's face was white and strained; the sweat was pouring down his forehead, but he dared not try to wipe it away. The glitter had faded from his bright eyes; they were glazed now with fear. He had never before met his match; he could not believe it, this must be impossible. He gathered himself for a last effort, but his chest was burning, his legs were weak, and his wrist was tiring.

Richard lunged, saw his opponent's blade sweep across, changed the line of his attack, feinted, saw an opening, and at the full stretch of long arm and long leg, drove his sword through de Marillac.

Richard stepped back. His whole body was shaking; his fingers were twitching, and as he rubbed his streaming face, he realized that he was drenched in perspiration, and that he was panting as if he had just run a frantic race for his life.

He looked at the untidy heap of coat and breeches sprawled out on the grass at his feet, the white face and the bared teeth, and then Richard's stomach heaved, and he was violently sick as he leant against a tree. If this was duelling, if this was 'killing your man', then he would never fight with swords again.

A strong hand supported him, and a deep voice muttered comforting remarks. 'We have been watching for several minutes,' Gribeauval said, 'but it was far too dangerous to interfere. He would have run you through if you had been distracted for even a second.'

Richard nodded; his head was clearing, and the sickness had gone.

'Who was he, *monsieur?*'

'One of the men at Graye-sur-Mer,' Richard said. 'I met him in London. The Vicomte de Marillac.'

'De Marillac!' Gribeauval's white head nodded continuously, as if that name explained everything. 'He had not forgotten, then. Now, Monsieur Carey, your arm is bleeding. Paul, see to this,' and he nodded towards the body on the grass. 'No one must know that he has ever been here.'

He led Richard towards the house.

'See if he has any papers on him,' he added to Paul over his shoulder.

'What will Paul do?' Richard asked.

'Bury him, *monsieur,*' Gribeauval said calmly, as if he made a practice of burying unwanted corpses in his garden. 'What about his friends? Are they in the village?'

'No. He said he was here on his own.'

'Ah, then we should be safe,' Gribeauval said as he unbuttoned Richard's coat and rolled up the sodden shirt-sleeve. 'Deep, Monsieur Carey, but clean.'

He shouted for the housekeeper, a silent woman who had asked no questions of Richard, and who made no comment now as she brought water and bandages.

'Hortense will say nothing,' Gribeauval said. 'She has been with us for twenty years.'

Richard winced as the bandage was tightened on his arm. 'How did de Marillac find us here?' he asked.

'Oh, he's a clever man,' Gribeauval said. 'He knows a great deal about the Assailly family, and his home is in Caen. He would ask himself where the Vicomte would go for shelter. To some faithful friend of the family, of course. In three days he could make many inquiries. He was bound to call at my house soon.'

He clicked his tongue as he saw the ruin of Richard's shirt and examined the rent in the coat-sleeve. 'Hortense can mend the coat for you, *monsieur*, but the shirt!' He shook his head. 'If we can find one large enough in this house, but I doubt it. Are they all mammoths in your family, Monsieur Carey?'

'Some of us,' Richard said. He thankfully drank the wine that Hortense had brought in; his throat was very dry after his tremendous exertions, and he was still feeling exhausted.

'I think you had better go up and reassure the Vicomte,' Gribeauval said. 'He will have heard the noise of the swords too.' He peered up at Richard with wondering eyes, and polished his spectacles vigorously.

Armand was sitting up in bed when Richard went into his room. His face was a picture of anxiety and impatience, for Armand never made any pretence of concealing his emotions, and Richard had already come to the conclusion that his cousin could not have done so if he had wished.

'What has been happening, Richard? You've been fighting! You're wounded! Who was it? . . .'

Richard sat down and leant back wearily, waiting for the flood of excited questions to end.

'It was one of the men on the beach at Graye-sur-Mer,' he said. 'I met him in London, and Father asked him for advice, as he knew this part of France. Unfortunately we didn't know he was an agent of the Republic.'

'But who was he, Richard?'

'The Vicomte de Marillac.'

Armand shot up in bed again. 'Charles de Marillac!' He sank back once more. 'That explains everything.'

'Well, it doesn't to me,' Richard said. 'Gribeauval said the same as you did. Who is this fellow, Armand?'

'De Marillac was a junior officer in Father's regiment,' Armand said. 'I don't know all the details, but he was cashiered for duelling, bad debts and some other scandals. He always had a pretty unsavoury reputation. Anyway, he blamed Father. It was he who denounced Father and had him arrested in Paris.'

Armand was tugging restlessly at the bedclothes, and then he started to get out of bed. Richard jumped up and pushed him back.

'For heaven's sake, stay where you are,' he said. 'What on earth are you trying to do, Armand?'

'We've got to leave here at once,' Armand said. 'Where's de Marillac now? Gone to fetch the others?'

'No. He's dead. And he was alone. So you're quite safe.'

'Dead! But I didn't hear a shot.'

'I ran him through with a small sword,' Richard said, and his mouth twitched.

Armand lay back again, but he was staring up at Richard in amazement. 'You ran Charles de Marillac through in a duel?' he said slowly. 'But that's impossible, Richard.'

The door opened, and Gribeauval came in, his wrinkled face beaming, a bundle of papers in his hand. Armand turned to him quickly.

'Is this true, Gribeauval? Did you see it?'

'I did, Monsieur le Vicomte. A counter-disengagement, a feint, and then a thrust in sixte.'

Armand whistled, and his eyes as they rested upon Richard were almost reverent in their respect. 'How long did the bout last?' he asked.

'About ten minutes,' Richard said, trying to visualize again those night-mare seconds when de Marillac was pressing home his attacks. 'He nearly got me several times. He was very fast, Armand.'

Armand's eyes twinkled. 'He was indeed, my dear Richard,' he said. 'But I still do not understand. I had not heard of your skill. They never mentioned you in the fencing salons as a master swordsman.'

'I'm not,' Richard said in surprise.

Armand sat up again and shook his finger at Richard. 'Charles de Marillac, and good riddance to him, has killed at least ten men to my knowledge. He was considered the most dangerous duellist in France.'

Richard shook his head in puzzlement. 'As good as that?' he said. 'I've been fencing a good deal lately with a French *émigré* in Cambridge, the Vicomte de Lessart, and old Loubet is in London now. But they have slowed down a lot, you know, Armand, and I couldn't go by that.'

Armand raised his clenched fists in the air. 'Henri de Lessart slow!' he cried in agony. 'Loubet! Old Loubet! Old! The greatest *maître d'armes* in Europe!' He collapsed dramatically again. 'Papa was quite correct when he described your family, my dear Richard. You are indeed the most exasper-ating, the most infuriating, the most solid lump of English beef . . .'

'Welsh,' Richard said, interrupting.

'Welsh or English, it matters not!' Armand cried. 'I say again, Richard, if you will kindly not interrupt, the most solid lump of Welsh beef I have ever met!'

'It's usually mutton in Wales,' Richard said, grinning at Armand's excited face. 'Good mutton, too. I could eat half a sheep now.' He shook his head sadly at his French cousin. 'That's the trouble with you French people,' he added. 'Too excitable. No control. Too emotional.'

'May heaven preserve me!' Armand said devoutly. 'Well, I suppose it runs in your family.'

'What does?' Richard asked suspiciously. 'Mutton?'

'No, your fencing!' Armand's voice rose to a squeak. 'They still speak reverently of your grandfather in the fencing salons. My own grandfather's greatest boast, apparently, was that he once fought a duel with the great Charles Carey.'

'What on earth did they fight about?'

'Who cares? They fought on the slightest provocation in those days.'

Gribeauval and Richard exchanged glances. Armand was looking white and strained after this excitement, and they persuaded him with difficulty to lie back and rest. Richard took the hint, and went downstairs to find Paul.

The garden was peaceful and quiet again, but Richard could see the marks of feet on the grass, and he shivered, despite the warm sun. His grandfather, he decided, could rest content with his duelling; his grandson had already had his fill of fencing.

The gate at the end of the garden clicked, and Richard dived into his pocket for a pistol. But it was Paul, shirt-sleeved and looking very hot.

'Well?' Richard asked.

'Very well, Monsieur Carey,' and Paul nodded grimly. 'I buried him in the wood outside. No one will ever find the grave.'

Richard blenched as he listened to Paul's matter-of-fact voice. He had prided himself on being such a man of the world, quite imperturbable, able to deal with any situation. But he had received so many shocks lately to his self-esteem that he knew now, with a most unusual humility, that he was a mere child, a beginner, a sheer amateur in this world of action.

Gribeauval came hurrying out of the house. He nodded his satisfaction at Paul's news, and flourished the papers which he was still holding.

'These were in de Marillac's pockets,' he said, and Richard took them from him gingerly. 'There is one appointing him as a representative of the Committee of Public Safety,' the old lawyer added. 'I should keep that, Monsieur Carey. It could be useful. You see, these special Representatives of the Committee are given unlimited powers. There are few people in France who would dare question anyone carrying that paper.'

Richard stuffed the papers into a pocket, and sat down on the garden seat with Gribeauval.

'What do we do next?' he asked hopelessly, a sure sign of how much he had lost his self-confidence. 'The Vicomte insists on going to Paris. Do you think there is anything he can do there to help his father?'

Gribeauval shook his head and began to polish his spectacles. 'Nothing, *monsieur*,' he said. 'And you? Will you return to England?'

'Oh, I don't know!' Richard said impatiently. 'I can't make up my mind.'

The old man looked at him and smiled; he resembled some very benevolent and wise old owl, and indeed he understood a great deal of the turmoil in Richard's mind, but he was far too intelligent to say much, or to give any advice. For this was something that Richard had to decide for himself.

But any decision was soon out of the question. The next morning found Armand in a high fever. The excitement of de Marillac's sudden appearance combined with his impatience to go to Paris were too much for him. Armand, as Richard had discovered, was not the most unemotional of young men. He made up his mind quickly and impulsively, he was excitable, even to Richard's colder nature, unstable, capable of jumping precipitately from one mood to another. One moment he would be depressed and moody, the next furiously happy and optimistic.

He was a bad patient, too, and his own temperament did not help. Rest and quiet were the best medicine for him, but they were the last things he was prepared to swallow. His wound became inflamed, and Gribeauval finally took the risk of sending for a doctor. His treatment of bleeding seemed to reduce the fever but left Armand extremely weak. Clearly he would not be able to leave the house for several weeks.

Richard began to fume. This inaction was something he had never faced before. He had read most of Gribeauval's books; he was tired of the confinement of the garden walls; the weather was fine and warm, and he eventually persuaded Paul to take him riding. They kept to the country roads, and they saw few people; Normandy was thinly populated, and there did not seem much danger.

They returned one evening to find Gribeauval waiting for them at the gate. 'A letter from England for you, Monsieur Carey,' he said. Richard snatched the letter. He was not altogether surprised. During the last few weeks old Rupert would have made a fresh plan. But the writing on the outside was in his father's neat hand, and was briefly addressed to 'The Hon. Richard Carey'.

Llanstephan Hall

My dear Richard,

I do not know if this will ever reach you. I am concerned for your safety, and blame myself for sending you into such danger. In the hope that my message may be delivered, the smuggler Price will bring his sloop to the beach three miles to the west of Graye-sur-Mer. There is a small cove there with no particular name, but there is a track leading to it from the village of Cresserons. Rupert considers it too risky to use the beach near Graye-sur-Mer. Price will be off the cove on each night during the last week of October.

I have made discreet inquiries from our Embassy in Paris, but they cannot guarantee a safe conduct for you. It would be wiser for you not to try and get in touch with them. De Marillac, it seems, is an agent of the new French Government. Loubet, the French *maître d'armes*, warned me of him the day after you left for Wales; I sent a letter to Rupert that morning, but you had sailed.

Price will try and send this letter to Vernaye in the hope that it may reach you. Amélie de Vernaye and Louise arrived safely, and are now at Llanstephan. Your mother and I pray for your safety, and Rupert is beside himself with anxiety. He would like to land in Normandy with an expeditionary force for your rescue.

Your affectionate father,
Aubigny

Richard smiled broadly as he read the final sentence about Rupert. There was nothing he would have liked better than to see that brisk little man stride into the garden, and take complete charge of the whole situation. He sighed; he would have to make his own plans, and he did not feel much confidence in his ability to do that. Anyway, there were three more weeks to go before Ianto Price would be off the coast again, and the first thing to do was to find the cove. Paul and Armand would be sure to know the best route.

Those three weeks passed with agonizing slowness. Armand was recovering again, but he was in no condition to travel. He was so weak that he could barely stagger across the room. To move him would be fatal, and Richard did not need the doctor's warning to see that for himself. So there was no possibility of taking Armand back to England this time.

Paul guided Richard to the cove near Cresserons. There was no moon, but the sky was clear, and it was a fairly warm October night. The sea was calm, and Richard felt no doubts this time, as Paul lighted their lantern and placed it on a high rock. If Ianto Price had said that he would be off this particular bay at this particular time, then he would indeed be there.

Richard sat on a flat rock and waited quite patiently and confidently. Paul, as usual, said nothing. Good or bad news came alike to his stolid nature, and he was a comforting sort of person to have with you, Richard decided.

'There, Monsieur Carey!' he said quietly. 'A light!'

Richard jumped to his feet and stumbled over the pebbles towards the water. He could see a boat now, and the two black oars on either side, rising on the crest of a wave, and shooting towards the beach. It grounded, and two men splashed through the shallow water.

One of them was the unmistakable figure of Ianto. But the other was much shorter, and Richard stared in amazement.

'Mr Carey?' came Ianto's shout. He was holding what looked like a blunderbuss, Richard thought, and he grinned. Ianto was taking no chances this time.

'Careful with that infernal weapon, Ianto!' a sharp, brisk voice barked. It was the short man speaking, a muffled figure in a long riding-coat, and a low-brimmed hat pulled down over his face. 'Point the damned thing out to sea, man! Fellow nearly blew my head off with one of those in the jungle one night!'

Richard stared again, and began to laugh.

'What the devil are you doing here, Rupert?' he asked.

9

Paris

'Hello, Richard,' Rupert said. 'Who's that with you? That's not Armand d'Assailly, surely?'

Richard explained the absence of Armand, while Rupert from his low height looked respectfully up at the gigantic figure of Paul. They were walking up the beach towards a small fisherman's hut that Paul had found, and which was deserted.

'No time to warn you about that fellow de Marillac,' Rupert said. 'Had a grudge against Quentin de Vernaye, you know. Somebody should have shot him years ago.'

'Well, he's dead now,' Richard said.

'What's that? You shot him, did you, boy? I told you those screw-barrel pistols of mine were . . .'

'I didn't kill him with a pistol, Rupert. With a small sword.'

Rupert whistled, and patted Richard on the shoulder. 'You've been keeping quiet about your fencing, my boy. De Marillac! The old man would have been proud of you.'

'What old man?' Richard asked. His uncle seldom kept to the point, he decided.

'Your grandfather, of course! Who else? This puts you in his class.'

'Class, what class, Rupert?'

'Your grandfather's! I said so, didn't I? Ianto, stand guard outside, and leave your lantern here. Now, get on with your story, and keep to the point!'

Richard swallowed and nodded as they sat down on two wooden cases on either side of a rough table that was frequently used for cutting up fish, to judge by the smell. Rupert laid down a pair of dangerous-looking pistols and peered at his nephew from under his low-brimmed hat, his face alive with vitality, his eyes sparkling. Quite clearly this trip to Normandy, the landing at night on a deserted beach, was a welcome change to him after his quiet life on the Gower coast. He was back again, if only for a short time, in the world of action.

He nodded as Richard finished his story. 'Armand's off to Paris, then, is he?' he said. 'Trying to rescue Quentin. Interesting, that could be. I can think of one possible . . . No, perhaps it would be easier to . . . Yes, I think I shall have to go with him.'

'You're going back to Wales,' Richard said firmly.

'It's devilish dull at Horton,' Rupert said pathetically. 'Don't like young Armand going off on his own,' he added, and he glanced across the table. His brisk voice had changed to a note of anxiety.

'He won't be alone,' Richard said. He had made up his mind at last.

'Oh,' said Rupert slowly. 'Won't he?'

'No, I'm going with him.' Richard drew a deep breath and waited for the inevitable storm of protests.

'I hoped you would say that, boy,' Rupert said. His hand gripped Richard's arm tightly for a moment, and the anxiety had vanished from his voice.

'Did you, indeed?'

'I've told you before,' Rupert snapped. 'You've got some strange ideas, my boy. We don't rat on our friends in our family, you know.'

He produced from the deep pocket of his coat a small canvas bag that clinked richly as he dropped it on the table. 'Guineas,' he said. 'Money's always useful in this kind of game. And two addresses in Paris.' He passed over a slip of paper. 'Two friends of mine. If they're still in Paris, they might be able to help you.'

Richard stuffed the bag into his pocket. 'You seem to have come pre-pared, Rupert.'

'Couldn't leave Quentin in the lurch,' Rupert said. 'If you weren't going to Paris, I was.'

Richard smiled. He was still learning a great deal about his uncle. For one moment he nearly begged Rupert to come to Paris too. But it was hardly fair.

'Do you think we've any chance of helping Uncle Quentin?' he asked.

Rupert hesitated. Then he shrugged his shoulders. 'About as much chance as persuading a Bengal tiger to eat out of your hand,' he said bluntly. 'Bribery's your main hope. Find the right man to bribe, and the worst is over. That's where these friends of mine may be able to help.'

Richard nodded gloomily. 'Tante Amélie arrived safely?' he asked. 'And Louise, too?' he added lamely.

Rupert peered at him in the uncertain light of the lanterns, and chuck-led. 'Pretty girl, isn't she?' he said, and he grinned as he saw Richard's expression. 'Sent you a message, boy. Told you to take care of yourself.'

'Did she say that?' Richard said eagerly.

'Yes, boy.' Rupert poked his nephew in the chest with the barrel of one of his pistols. 'So that's how the land lies, eh?' And he laughed.

'Is that pistol cocked, Rupert?' Richard asked, and he pushed the long barrel out of the way. 'Well, give her my . . . Send her my regards, Rupert.'

'What, no letter for her?' Rupert said. 'Bit slow, aren't you, my boy? Well, you leave it to me. And I'll be your best man at the wedding.' He kicked away the box on which he had been sitting. 'Look after yourself,

Richard. I thought you'd turn out well. Now, if I'd had you in the Carnatic with me in '61, we should have done famously together.' He patted Richard affectionately on the shoulder, and they went outside to the darkness and the lonely cove and the wash of the sea.

Rupert splashed his way to the boat, cursed bitterly in Hindustani as a wave came over the top of his boots, and hunched himself up in the stern with Ianto.

Richard stood on the sand, oblivious of the water swirling around his feet, until he could no longer see the boat. Then he turned and walked slowly up the beach to where Paul was waiting with the horses. Richard felt extremely lonely once more, but he was happier now. He had made up his mind; he knew what he had to do, though he did not feel particularly confident of any success. It was odd, he was thinking as they trotted up the track from the sea, that it was Rupert's praise that had pleased him most. He had always taken praise and deference for granted so far in his life. But it was something new to learn that in many things he still had to earn respect from other people.

Richard and Armand left for Paris a week after Christmas. They had wanted to ride, but Gribeauval had told them that horses would make them much too conspicuous. Far better and safer for them to travel by the ordinary diligence from Caen to Paris, and their role could be that of two university students returning for their next term.

Papers of identity had been the greatest difficulty, but Gribeauval had solved that problem too, by bribery and forgery, and with the help of the local officials. So it was as Richard Carrier and Armand Roland, two cousins from Colombey-sur-Thaon, that they rode into Caen.

The journey to Paris lasted for four days. The weather was appalling, with chilly rain falling persistently from the low clouds. The diligence was an enormous and cumbersome vehicle that bumped and swayed and lurched and crashed over the rough *pavé* at a steady four miles to the hour. Richard sat in his corner seat, cold, bored and depressed, watching the sodden countryside that moved slowly past the window. Accustomed to the trim, well-kept fields of England, he was surprised to see how primitive French farming was. But there was nothing else to see except the straight, interminable roads lined with trees, the heavy clouds and the unceasing, persistent rain.

The inns at which they stopped for meals were filthy and ridden with vermin, and the food was atrocious; the other passengers in the coach were silent and seemed to avoid questions; apparently few people dared to express their opinions about politics or, indeed, about any other matter. It was safer, Richard gathered, to hold your tongue.

Huddled in the thin, cheap overcoat suitable for a poor student, Richard rubbed his unshaven chin and yearned for a bath and a good hot meal. The others who boarded the diligence at the various stages had presumably not washed for months, he thought bitterly, and it was a relief when the coachman asked them to alight and walk up the steeper hills.

And then at last they reached Paris. But there were no prosperous suburbs, as Richard was used to seeing outside London, and little traffic; even the occasional large house was deserted or burnt out.

The diligence lurched to a standstill outside a tall, forbidding gateway. A group of soldiers in dirty uniforms lounged outside the guardhouse, and one of them slouched forward towards the coach. He opened the door, thrust his grimy, unshaven face inside, and scowled at the passengers.

'Your papers,' he growled.

Richard handed over his papers with the others, and sat back against the worn upholstery with an air of utter unconcern. But his knees were shaking, and his fists were clenched convulsively inside his pockets. He tried not to shiver at the icy draughts that blew in through the open door, and he shot a quick glance at Armand. Armand was sitting tensely, too, or so Richard noticed, for he knew his French cousin by this time.

The sergeant handed back the papers, nodded to the coachman and growled an order to the men at the gate. Gribeauval was right, then, Richard decided. To enter Paris was a fairly simple matter; to leave was very different.

The diligence rumbled over the cobbles, through narrow, winding streets ankle deep in mud, with dilapidated old houses rearing up on either side, topped with pointed roofs and oddly shaped gables. At regular intervals ancient lanterns swayed and creaked in the wind, and all around swarmed the Parisians, dodging the many carts that crashed over the uneven road in a bedlam of noise that made Richard's head ache.

They alighted outside an inn and collected their canvas bags from the boot. Richard stretched his long legs and wondered if he would be able to have a bath that night. He shivered in the icy wind; the sky was a steely grey, the *pavé* was coated with ice, and the date, as he read on a newspaper by the inn door, was 5 January 1793.

'Keep your head down, Richard,' Armand muttered. 'Don't look round so curiously.'

Richard nodded and did as he was told, though he did not think that anyone would take much notice of them in those crowded streets. He followed Armand's hurrying figure, and they came out into a wide square.

'Place de Carousel,' Armand said, and he increased his pace.

In the centre of the square was a high wooden platform, and on it stood two tall posts with a heavy cross-piece. The wood was a dull red, and the fading light glinted for a second on the great steel blade hanging from the cross-piece. There was a stark simplicity and a brooding air of menace about that platform and the dark red timbers that made Richard shiver again, and Armand, who had taken one glance at the guillotine, turned his head and dived down another street.

'Rue St Honoré,' he said. 'We want Number 237. That's at the other end, I think.'

Richard said nothing. He was colder than ever, and he felt faintly sick after the fear that had swept over him at the barrier, and the stuffy smell of those long hours in the diligence. He was hungry, too, and now they had ahead of them the worry of wondering if Monsieur Duport would help them. He was a tailor, a fashionable one in the old days, and had made clothes for the Marquis. Like Gribeauval, so Armand said, he was devoted to the Assailly family, for he had received many kindnesses from them, and had originally come from Normandy, where his father had been a tenant of the Marquis.

The street was wider and lined with shops, a much more prosperous area than that through which they had entered Paris. There were few people about, for the light was failing, and many of the shops were already closed.

'Here we are!' Armand said, and he stopped in front of a tailor's window. To the side was a neat, green-painted door, and Armand rapped on it quietly. Richard hunched his shoulders and shivered as the biting wind went through his miserable coat. He should never have allowed old Gribeauval to take away his shooting-coat, but the lawyer had pointed out that, old as it was, it was far too luxurious for a university student.

Armand rapped again, louder this time. Richard grew even more depressed as he looked down the street, dark now, and unwelcome. This feeling of being homeless, of not knowing where you could sleep that night, was one that he had never experienced before. He was indeed a fool, he thought. By this time he could have been lounging in front of a roaring fire in the library at Llanstephan, well dressed, clean and sleepy after an excellent dinner. Or he might even have been sitting in the Mediterranean sun with Rupert, with no worries and . . .

'Yes, *messieurs?*' a high-pitched, childish voice said behind him.

The green door had been opened by a dark-haired little girl, with a pert, inquiring face that framed an upturned nose and an expression of mischief in the shrewd eyes that inspected the two young men before her.

'Monsieur Duport?' Armand said.

'Papa is doing his accounts,' she said. 'Your name, *monsieur?*'

'Would you tell your papa that we are from Colombey-sur-Thaon?' Armand said, and he smiled down at her. Armand's smile was a charming one, and the little girl appeared to think so too, for she smiled back, skipped inside the hall, and waved a hand for them to follow.

Richard went inside thankfully, and they waited in the hall until the girl reappeared, and held open a door on the left. Armand smiled at her again, and they found themselves in a small office, crowded with rolls of cloth, an untidy, warm and comfortable place after the cold street outside. A bright fire burnt cheerfully, and a man was standing behind the desk in the corner.

He was grey-haired and plump, with rosy cheeks and the same upturned nose as his little daughter; a quietly dressed and prosperous-looking man, for his coat, so Richard noticed, was of fine cloth well cut.

'Yes, *messieurs?*' he asked with a note of caution in his voice. His sharp eyes flickered over Richard and then turned to Armand, assessing the price and quality of their clothes in one sweeping, professional glance. But the grey eyebrows rose slightly as they rested on Armand's face, and the smooth forehead wrinkled.

'We are friends of Monsieur Edouard Gribeauval of Colombey-sur-Thaon,' Armand said. 'We . . .'

The tailor smiled. 'You are very like your father, Monsieur le Vicomte,' he said.

'My father!' Armand leant across the desk. 'How is he? Do you know where he is? Is he still alive, Duport?'

Duport held up a white, plump hand. 'Calm yourself, *monsieur*,' he said. 'The Marquis is in good health. I saw him five days ago.'

'You saw him! How did you manage that?'

'Quite simply. Friends and relations are still allowed to visit some of the prisoners occasionally. A little money helps, of course. Please be seated, *messieurs*.'

Richard took the chair nearest the fire, and held out his numbed hands to the cheerful glow. But Armand was still asking his impatient, anxious questions.

'He is in good health, you said?'

'Oh, yes, *monsieur*. He is in the Abbaye prison, and that is the best of the Paris prisons, though that is not saying much. They have mattresses there, and there are not more than six prisoners to a room. Far better than the Châtelet or the Conciergerie.'

He looked inquiringly at Richard, and Armand explained quickly who Richard was.

'Carey?' the tailor said. 'I think I remember a relation of yours, Monsieur Carey. He came here with the Marquis, and I made him a coat. A Sir Carey . . . I am not very good at your English titles. Ah, yes, Sir Rupert! He wanted a special pocket in the coat.'

Richard grinned. 'What for?'

'A pistol, *monsieur*. Yes, Sir Carey knew exactly what he wanted. And I have not so easily forgotten him, you see.'

No, Richard thought, Rupert was not a man you forgot quickly. But Armand had listened impatiently to this chatter of pockets and pistols. Once his mind had fixed itself on any subject, then he pursued it with a determination that no one could shake.

'I shall go and see my father tomorrow,' he said.

'You must do nothing of the kind!' the tailor said urgently. 'It would be fatal. Your name is on the list of those denounced as enemies of the Republic.'

'Oh!' Armand said blankly. He sat down on the nearest chair with a crash. 'What are we to do, then? Sit here until he is executed? I could see him then, of course, as he climbs the steps to the guillotine.'

The tailor shrugged his shoulders. 'Escape is difficult now,' he said. 'Last year things were different; the prisons were overcrowded and not well guarded. But now . . .' and his white hands spread themselves out in apology.

Armand grunted impatiently; he clenched his hands and turned hopefully to Richard, who shook his head.

'Let's have some food, Armand,' he said.

'Food!' Armand exclaimed. 'Food!'

Duport touched his arm. 'Yes, you will feel better then, Monsieur le Vicomte. And a good night's rest.'

By the following morning Armand was more optimistic, which did not surprise Richard. Armand rushed violently from one mood to another, and the moods were as violent as the rapid changes. In comparison Richard felt that he was as cool and composed a person as any man in Paris.

'I'm going to call on some friends,' Armand said. 'If any of them are still in Paris. Will you come, Richard?'

Richard was looking at the sheet of paper that Rupert had given him. 'I think I'll call on these people,' he said. 'How do I find them, Armand? The first name is Georges Lamourette, 55 Rue de Vaugirard.'

'On the south bank,' Armand said. 'Near the Palace of the Luxemburg.'

'And Robert Hervilly, 27 Rue St Antoine.'

'That's close to the old Bastille, or what's left of it. Won't you wait and let me come with you, Richard?'

'Oh, I'll be all right,' Richard said. 'My French will pass, won't it?'

Richard walked briskly through the crowded, narrow streets. No one stopped to stare at him, though he felt that he must be a conspicuous figure, and at any moment he expected a rough hand to seize his arm. After the first ten minutes or so he felt safer, and then he realized that there was no possible reason for alarm. Who in Paris knew him by sight? The only man who could have identified him was dead and buried near the garden of old Gribeauval.

He asked his way several times, but his French was fluent and his accent too slight to attract attention. The Rue de Vaugirard, when he found it, was muddy and dirty, with old houses that were badly in need of repair; the windows and doors needed paint, and the few people about were equally dirty and unpleasant. Not the area in which a friend of Rupert's would live, Richard thought uneasily. But then Rupert's acquaintances were a pretty mixed lot, and now that he was here, he might as well see this Monsieur Lamourette.

He knocked at the door of Number 55, and it was opened immediately by a bent old man in a rusty black coat who peered suspiciously and a trifle uneasily at Richard.

'Monsieur Lamourette?' Richard asked.

The old man looked up and down the street, and pulled Richard inside the house into a hall that smelt of cooking; the walls were damp, and the wallpaper was peeling away in long strips.

'Who are you?' the man asked, looking up into Richard's face.

'Just a friend of Monsieur Lamourette.'

'But don't you know?'

'Know what?' Richard asked sharply.

'He was arrested last week.'

'What for?'

The bent shoulders lifted in a shrug of helplessness. 'Who asks that these days, *monsieur?* Enemy of the Republic. That's enough.'

Richard sighed. That left him with one hope only now, Robert Hervilly. He turned towards the door, but the old man caught him by the arm.

'Times are hard, *monsieur*,' he said plaintively. 'Very hard, *monsieur.*'

Richard hesitated. Young men wearing the cheap clothes that he had on his back would be unlikely to have much money in their pockets. But he pushed a handful of assignat notes into the shaking hand, and walked away quickly.

The Rue St Antoine was on the north bank, so Richard retraced his steps, another long walk through the muddy streets with their clatter of carts and the pushing, swarming crowds. The Rue St Antoine was wider than most, and Richard's hopes rose as he saw that the houses were reasonably new and infinitely more respectable than those of the Rue Vaugirard.

The concierge was old, but clean and polite, though he seemed oddly nervous when Richard asked for Monsieur Hervilly.

'He is out, *monsieur.*'

'When will he be back?'

The man's eyes shifted, stared at Richard's boots, then at the wall behind him. 'Not today, *monsieur.* He is out of Paris.'

'Well, will he be back tomorrow?'

'Oh, yes, *monsieur*, certainly. If you would call . . .' The man hesitated and shuffled his feet. 'If you were to call at five o'clock, *monsieur?*'

Richard nodded. Why on earth was the man frightened, he wondered uneasily, because there was fright behind those shifting eyes and those shuffling feet.

'I'll call at five,' he said, and he left the house. Perhaps most people in Paris were frightened or uneasy, he decided, as he returned to the Rue St Honoré.

Armand had already returned and was sitting in front of the fire in Monsieur Duport's little office. One look at his despondent figure was enough for Richard. So Armand had had an unsuccessful morning, too.

'No luck?' he asked Richard.

'No. And you?'

'All my friends have left the country,' Armand said. 'Even Charles de Talleyrand has gone.'

'Do you mean the Bishop of Autun?' Richard asked, and there was a note of contempt in his voice, for the Bishop's reputation was not a savoury one.

'Oh, you'd soon change your mind about Charles if you met him,' Armand said.

'Possibly,' Richard said doubtfully. 'I didn't know you were one of his friends, Armand.'

'I went to his house a good deal. We talked politics. But we didn't want all this to happen. Why, I heard today that they are going to try the King!'

'What did you want to happen?' Richard asked curiously.

He listened to the torrent that rushed from Armand, the plans they had discussed for the reform of the Government; none of it sounded very revolutionary to Richard, accustomed to a Parliamentary Government in England. He was faintly surprised, though, to realize that Armand was one of the moderate reformers. He was pleased, too, for his father had often spoken scathingly about the inefficiency and corruption of the old regime in France.

They ate lunch with the Duport family, and the tailor told Richard that he had delivered a message for him at the British Embassy. As he was making a suit of clothes for one of the staff, his visit would not arouse any suspicion, and Richard himself was following his father's advice to keep clear. But Rupert had said that large funds had been deposited there in Richard's name for him to call upon if he needed them, and it seemed a sensible idea to let the Embassy know that he was now in Paris.

'They are sending someone round here this afternoon, Monsieur Carey. He is due to be measured for a pair of breeches in any case, and he said he wished to have a word with you.'

There was certainly nothing else he could do, Richard thought gloomily. If Hervilly could not help him, then they had indeed come to Paris on a hopeless gamble. The trouble would be to persuade Armand of that; Richard knew now how obstinate he could be.

Soon after three o'clock Duport ushered a gentleman into the office.

'Monsieur Lilley to see you, Monsieur Carey,' he said.

Lilley was an elegant and dignified man, about ten years older than Richard, very sure of himself, and somewhat condescending, as if he were conferring a considerable favour on Richard by consenting to see him at all.

Richard stirred in his chair. He was not used to this tone of voice, and he watched Lilley seat himself with a flick of his smart coat-tails, look around the untidy little room, and then pull out a snuff-box.

'Snuff, Mr Carey?' he asked in a precise and fluty voice.

'No, thank you. I believe my father has sent you a letter of credit on my behalf?'

'Yes, that is so. I am surprised that Lord Aubigny, who knows the position in Paris, should have permitted you to leave England and come to France, Mr Carey.'

Richard stiffened angrily. Lilley might be a professional diplomat, the heir to a baronetcy, but who the devil did he think he was to question what the Carey family might do, or why?

'Our official position in Paris is very delicate,' Lilley said. He took snuff delicately, too, with an elegant flick of his fingers. 'I believe you are still at Cambridge, Mr Carey, so perhaps you do not realize how embarrassing it would be if you came to us for help. Relations between His Majesty's Government and that of France are strained – devilish strained, I may say.'

'I'm not asking you for any help,' Richard said curtly.

'Very wise of you, Mr Carey. There is nothing we could do, in any case.' He glanced at Armand, who did not understand this swift flow of English. 'The Marquis de Vernaye is in prison, and the Vicomte is liable to be arrested on sight. So, too, are you, Mr Carey.'

Richard fought down his rising temper. So the line this pompous tailor's dummy was taking was that of the experienced man of the world, the trained diplomat, delivering a lecture to an ignorant young undergraduate. Was he still at Cambridge, indeed! Didn't he know that relations between the new Republic and Great Britain were strained!

'Why should I be arrested?' he asked, controlling himself with an effort.

'Because of the activities of the Vicomte de Marillac. People talked very freely to him in London, and he came back with a great deal of useful information. I have no doubt that your name was given by him to his new masters, Mr Carey.'

'Well, no one knows me by sight in Paris,' Richard said.

'But de Marillac does.' Lilley took another pinch of snuff, and his prominent blue eyes ran over Richard's shabby clothes.

'De Marillac is dead,' Richard said curtly. He had noticed that slightly contemptuous inspection.

'Indeed, Mr Carey. How did you learn that?' Lilley was interested now.

'He followed us from the coast to the house in which we were hiding. At a village called Colombey-sur-Thaon. He and I fought with small swords, and I killed him.'

Mr Lilley stared at Richard in astonishment, shaken out of his supercilious attitude; the astonishment gave way to respect. Young and inexperienced men, mere undergraduates, never fought and killed swordsmen with an international reputation. At least, not in Mr Lilley's experience. He remembered, a trifle belatedly, that Richard's father was a member of the Government, and that the Carey family might have good friends, and powerful ones too, and that they were a dangerous and closely knit family group when their own members were threatened.

'I will let you know if I want any of that money,' Richard said. 'And don't be afraid that I shall embarrass you, Mr Lilley. Now, I believe that Monsieur Duport has a coat ready for you.'

Lilley was on his feet, though he was not quite certain how he had got there. He bowed. 'Er, yes, Mr Carey. You understand that my position, and that of the Embassy . . .'

'Perfectly,' Richard said. He opened the door. 'Good afternoon, Mr Lilley.'

Richard drew a deep breath. He watched Lilley close the door, and then he laughed. He had lost his temper badly, but that brief outburst had done him good.

A thin rain was falling when Richard came down to breakfast the next morning. Armand was still in bed, and he would probably stay there for another hour at least. His mood was now one of complete despair; there was no hope for his father, he was convinced, and Richard felt much the same. Their last hope was the unknown Monsieur Hervilly, and they would know how valuable he might be that evening when Richard paid his five o'clock call. Meanwhile there was a long and boring day to be passed somehow and in this weather Richard decided to find a book and spend the time in front of Duport's fire.

The same concierge greeted him in the Rue St Antoine. His manner was even more nervous than before, and Richard inspected him curiously, and with a growing uneasiness.

'What is wrong?' he asked. 'You're frightened of something?'

'But no, *monsieur*, no! What could be wrong? It is just that everyone in Paris is frightened these days.'

'I suppose so,' Richard said doubtfully. 'On which floor is Monsieur Hervilly to be found?'

'The third, *monsieur*. The door on your left when you reach the landing.'

Richard went up the stairs slowly. There was something wrong. He felt it instinctively. That was something that Rupert had told him, too. You learn to smell danger, he had said; at least, some fortunate men did, and they were fools unless they took precautions. What precautions could he take, Richard wondered? He had a pistol in each pocket. He slid his hands inside the pockets and fingered the smooth butts; the mere touch reassured him, and he quickened his pace.

He hesitated outside the door on the third landing, then shrugged his shoulders, and tapped on the panel.

'*Entrez!*' a voice said from inside.

Richard walked inside, and the door was slammed behind him with a crash. Richard whirled round. A man was leaning back against the door, and he smiled at the startled expression on Richard's face.

Slowly Richard turned. Another man was standing by the window. In the fading light it was difficult to see their faces under the brims of their hats; both wore dark coats and white breeches with top boots; in each buttonhole was a rosette, and round each waist was a coloured sash.

There was no need for Richard to ask them who they were. He knew quite well. They were Government agents. He had walked into a neat trap.

10

Mr Bellamy

All three stared at each other for a moment in silence. After the first shock Richard's brain had recovered very quickly, and he was able to think about his next move. He must get away, that was quite clear. Once arrested, there would be little chance for him. Both the men were armed, with heavy pistols stuck into the sashes around their waists. Not very easy to pull one out quickly, Richard thought. But even if he reached one man in time, and knocked him down, the other could shoot him at leisure.

'Yes, Citizen?' said the man at the window.

'I came to see a Monsieur Robert Hervilly.' Richard decided to brazen it out.

'Citizen Hervilly,' the man said, with a slight emphasis on the 'Citizen'. 'Citizen Hervilly was arrested last week. And why do you wish to see an enemy of the Republic?'

'I'm a university student,' Richard said. 'From Colombey-sur-Thaon in Normandy. I've never met Citizen Hervilly. But he is an acquaintance of my uncle, Edouard Gribeauval, and he asked me to call on Citizen Hervilly.'

The man by the window, obviously the senior of the two, digested this story; he was a short, stumpy fellow, with a white and haggard face. The man by the door was short, too, but fairly stout, with a vacant, somewhat stupid face. He leant against the door and was listening indifferently to

the conversation, but his eyes were on Richard.

'Your name, Citizen?'

'Richard . . . Cartier.' Richard hesitated for a fraction of a second over the name; he had never been asked for it before, and it did not come easily to his tongue.

'You do not seem very certain of that, Citizen,' the Frenchman said. 'Your papers.'

Richard pulled out his papers and put them on the table. He would have to watch this fellow; he had been quick enough to notice that momentary hesitation. The agent bent down to read the documents. Richard had moved two steps closer to him when he had asked for the papers, and with his long reach, Richard could have touched him at arm's length now.

'I am not satisfied, Citizen,' the man said, and he raised his head. 'You will come with us.'

Richard's right caught him on the chin with a smack. He went over on his back, and the small table with him, and Richard span round with all the agility and speed of the trained fencer. Oh for my sword, he thought, as he leapt for the man at the door.

But his risk had been a calculated one; he had been relying on that expression of stupidity on the man's face, and he had been right. The second agent had gaped for the first vital second when his companion went down, and only when Richard was nearly on him did he snatch at his pistol.

He had tugged it out when Richard's hand closed on his wrist, and the other came up in a blurred white streak and crunched into his jaw. He went back against the door, and Richard swung viciously once more. As the man went down, he reached for the door-knob and pulled.

But although the door opened, it jammed against the man lying on the floor; there was barely room for Richard to squeeze through. He grunted, and some instinct made him turn and drop to his knees. The first agent was struggling to his feet, pistol in hand. There was a bright flash and a tremendous explosion, magnified in that small room, and the bullet thudded into the door above Richard's head.

Richard turned again, felt a hand grasp for his feet, kicked out wildly, and was through the door, which he pulled behind him. And there was the key on the outside, as the two agents had left it. Richard turned it, and rushed across the landing and down the stairs in a clatter of feet. That shot would fetch the concierge; no wonder he had been so scared, acting under orders from two Government agents. Richard pulled out a pistol; he was not going to be stopped now, and once he reached the street he could easily escape into the darkness, for the sun was down, and the hanging lanterns of Paris did not give much light.

He thundered down to the landing below. A door opened, and a hand caught at him. Up came Richard's pistol, but it was not cocked. Too late now, and the dark figure in the doorway grasped his wrist.

'Quick, Carey!' the figure said in English. 'Through here! They've got two men downstairs in the hall!'

He pulled Richard through the open door, and pushed him across a darkened room. Richard stumbled over a chair, then kicked it out of his way.

'Through the window!' hissed the voice behind him. 'Ten-foot drop only.'

Richard was not conscious of any coherent thought. He did as he was told instinctively. He thrust his long legs clumsily through the window, wriggled his body out until he was hanging by his fingers to the sill, his feet scrabbling for a hold. But there was none.

'Let yourself go,' the voice said above his head. 'Bend your knees, and roll when you hit the ground!'

Richard drew a deep breath and let go. But there was no time to worry about bending his knees in that swift drop. His feet smashed into the ground with a jar that went through his whole body, and he sprawled clumsily on the ground, half winded and wondering if he had broken a leg. A thud and a heavy body rolled over on him. A hand tugged urgently at his coat-sleeve.

'Quick, Carey! This way!'

Richard scrambled to his feet. Two dark figures were bending over him, and a new voice hissed at him.

'Down the alley there!' it said, and Richard pounded after the two men in the darkness, slipping and stumbling on the muddy cobbles, past blank, shuttered windows, under the creaking, swaying lanterns with their pools of yellow light, round a corner, then another, through the labyrinth of alleys and streets that honeycombed the poorer parts of Paris.

Richard was panting loudly when they pulled up in front of a tall house, and he was pulled inside a dark hall, one hand guiding him through a door until he found himself sitting on a hard chair, head down and gasping for breath.

'Can you hear anything, Jack?' a voice asked.

Richard heard the rasp of flint, and a candle flickered, throwing a narrow circle of light over the table. But Richard was wondering where he had heard that voice before. One of the men was holding back the window curtain, and the other was standing by the door. From him came a crack, and then another crack as he tugged uneasily at his fingers.

Richard held up the candle. 'Bellamy!' he said. 'Where the devil did you jump from?'

The second man had lighted another candle, and Richard could see Bellamy clearly now. The man's long, sallow face broke into a smile as he watched Richard.

'Oh, I've been in Paris for over a year, Mr Carey. Put some wood on the fire, Jack. I'm frozen, even after that run. By the way, Mr Carey, may I introduce you to Jack Wilson?'

Richard nodded his head; he was still far too bewildered by everything that had happened in the last few minutes. He watched the two men as they lighted candles, made up the fire and put food on the table.

Bellamy had not changed much since he had seen him last in Cambridge. He was still small, thin and clumsy, and his black hair hung down over his high forehead as untidily as ever. But his nervousness had gone; so too had those irritating repetitions at the end of each sentence.

Wilson was a powerful young man with wide shoulders and large, capable hands. But to describe him would have been difficult, for though Richard could have said that he possessed a nose, a mouth and two eyes, he could not have added that there was anything conspicuous about them, unusual or usual. His face was just a blank, and as he seldom spoke, Richard often forgot that the man was in the room at all. Jack Wilson merely faded into the background, and that, so it seemed, was his main object.

They set cold meat in front of him, some rough wine, bread and cheese, and apologized for the food. Richard ate hungrily. There were many questions he would like to have asked, but both men were behaving as if the events of the last hour were of no importance. When he had finished, he turned to Bellamy.

'Look here, Bellamy,' he said.

Bellamy laughed. 'You want to know how Jack and I arrived so providentially, eh?'

'I certainly do.'

'Well, it's quite simple, really. We are agents for the British Foreign Office. Unofficial ones, and not connected with the Embassy in any way. They know about us, but I don't think they approve.'

Richard grinned. He could not imagine the pompous Mr Lilley approving of either Bellamy or Wilson.

'Our main job is to collect information,' Bellamy said, 'send reports of public opinion in Paris, possible moves by the Government. Most of the stuff we send to London is unimportant. But occasionally we do learn something useful, not often, but enough to make it worth our while.'

'But what were you doing at Hervilly's apartment?' Richard asked.

'He is one of our sources of information. I think he is almost certainly acting under orders from the *émigrés* in Germany. The King's brother, the Duke of Artois, is at their head. Anyway, Hervilly was arrested a couple of days ago, and we noticed that two agents of the Republic were watching the house. Our job was to stop our friends from going inside, in case they were arrested too. Jack here saw you talking to the concierge yesterday. He didn't know who you were, but we decided to speak to you tonight. But you were too early for us. I saw you go in, and I couldn't believe my eyes, Mr Carey. I had no idea you were in Paris. We went in by the back door, and heard the shot, and saw you come out. That's when Jack grabbed you.'

Richard finished his red wine – pretty poor stuff, he thought, but he was thirsty after his exertions.

'We would like to know one thing, Mr Carey,' Bellamy said. His quiet, assured manner made Richard smile. 'What are you doing in Paris?'

Richard explained, and the two men listened in silence; they asked no questions, but there was little either of them had missed, Richard thought. Bellamy tugged at his fingers when Richard had finished, and exchanged glances with the silent Mr Wilson.

'We should have known about this man de Marillac,' Bellamy said. 'Did you take any papers from him?'

'The usual identity ones, and his special pass as an agent of the Committee of Public Safety.'

'Ah, now that might be useful, Mr Carey. The other point that puzzles me is how did you know about Hervilly?'

'I didn't know anything about him. My uncle, Sir Rupert, gave me his address, and said that he might be able to help us.'

'Sir Rupert!' Bellamy smiled, and his fingers cracked with delight. 'Well, that solves all our problems, Mr Carey. Do you think you can find your way back to the Rue St Honoré? Perhaps Jack had better come with you. Safer not to ask the way at night in Paris these days.'

He stood up, and Richard did the same instinctively; but then he sat down again. 'Look here, Bellamy,' he said. 'We want help, Armand d'Assailly and I. You are just the people.'

Bellamy shook his head regretfully. 'No, no, Mr Carey. I was afraid you would say that. We can do nothing to help you.'

Richard glared at him indignantly. 'But why not?' he demanded.

'We have quite definite orders. On no account must we become involved with escapes from the prisons, or any plots against the Government. Our duty is to report, and nothing else.'

Richard grunted. There was a note of polite and very firm refusal in Bellamy's voice. 'Can't you even suggest anything?' he pleaded, and the mere thought that he was begging favours from the despised Bellamy made him wriggle his feet uneasily.

Bellamy exchanged glances with Wilson, who was sitting on the other side of the fire, perfectly still, his face a blank, and indifferent to the whole conversation, or so he seemed, though Richard felt that the man had probably missed nothing.

He shook his head slightly at Richard. 'We'll think about it, Mr Carey,' he said. 'Not easy, you know.'

'Anyway, you know where to find us,' Bellamy said. 'But you must not come here unless it is really urgent. You understand that, Mr Carey?'

Richard nodded meekly. He was being lectured by Bellamy now. But the fellow had changed in the most extraordinary manner; there was a certain force and directness about him that impressed Richard, despite his annoyance at being impressed at all.

Wilson led him back through the maze of dark streets to the Rue St Honoré. Beyond an occasional curt instruction about the various turnings they took, he said nothing, and when he was satisfied that Richard could safely be left, he nodded and disappeared into the gloom. Led like a child by a nursemaid, Richard thought angrily, as he hurried down the street; these two men were treating him in the way a trained and experienced professional agent would condescend towards a bumbling amateur. With a shock, Richard realized that this was indeed the position. To Bellamy he was probably a nuisance and a danger, stumbling clumsily around Paris, attempting an impossible task with blundering inefficiency.

For the next two days Armand went the rounds of his friends, though without any success; many of them were no longer in Paris, and those who were had no intention of risking their lives by trying to help Armand in what they considered a hopeless and dangerous task. All they wished to do was to remain in safe obscurity, and Richard could not help sympathizing with them. The effect of all this on Armand was to reduce him to a state of bitter depression, and the news that the Convention had finally voted for the execution of the King only made matters worse.

Paris was quiet on that third day, and Duport advised them to stay indoors, though Richard was anxious to go out. He was finding this confinement and lack of action intolerably boring. But he joined Duport and Armand at the upstairs windows of the tailor's house as the street outside gradually filled with a restless and excited crowd of Parisians.

'They are taking no chances,' Armand said. 'National Guards all along the pavements.'

'I have never seen so many troops in the streets before,' Duport said. 'Every barrier out of the city is manned with a double guard, I was told.'

Richard watched the crowd; it was not a hostile one, he thought, just curious and somewhat subdued, waiting patiently in the chill mist that hung over Paris.

'What's that?' he asked, cocking his head.

'Drums,' Armand said.

From the left, far down the road, came the steady throb of sound, and then the drummers outside took up the monotonous beat, a dull, forbidding roll that filled Richard with a feeling of depression and fear.

Then he heard a different sound, the clip-clop of many hooves, and a squadron of cavalry trotted past; the crowds swayed and pushed, and fell silent. Richard craned his head out of the window. But there was little to see, except the dense masses of horsemen, and in the centre a large green coach that rumbled swiftly over the cobbles. Richard caught a brief glimpse of a brown-coated man inside, a calm, white face and a high forehead, and King Louis had passed.

'Close the window,' Armand said harshly.

He went and sat by the fire, poking at the coals with his boot. Outside the drums had fallen silent, but they were still beating in the distance, and the sound suddenly increased, and then abruptly they stopped, while all Paris waited. For a minute Richard raised his head, and Armand crouched by the fire. Then the drums rolled out once more for a few seconds, stopped again, and Armand sighed heavily, and dropped his head, his long fingers covering his face.

Armand refused to move from the house all the next day, but Richard was determined to go out. He had no idea what to do next; he could see no solution to any of their problems. The chances of helping Quentin d'Assailly were obviously quite hopeless, and the best thing that he and Armand could do would be to try to leave France. Even that would be difficult, but the effort would at least give them something to do, instead of hiding like rats in Duport's house.

Duport had suggested that Richard should go and listen to the debates in the Convention; they met daily in the old Riding School of the Tuileries Palace, the tailor said, and there was no risk attached to such a visit. No papers were asked for in the public gallery, and foreigners and visitors to Paris went there out of curiosity, for the Convention was one of the sights of Paris now.

Duport was right, for Richard walked in with several other people through the door that led to the public gallery; nobody stopped them, or showed the slightest interest as Richard found an empty seat on a wooden bench, and looked about him curiously.

He was looking down at a long and narrow room lit by windows high up on the walls. Rows of green leather seats rose on either side of a gangway that ran the full length of the chamber, so that the speakers faced each other, as did the members in the English House of Commons.

But there all similarity vanished. The members spoke, as Richard saw, from a kind of pulpit, and there was already a speech in progress. Richard leant forward to listen. But if he was expecting a vivid, sparkling debate such as he had often heard at Westminster, he was disappointed, for the speaker was reading his speech, a rambling, dull and extremely vague lecture on the present system of taxation in France. The other members seemed to share Richard's boredom, for few were listening; dressed in long overcoats, they strolled about, chatted loudly and ignored completely the continual ringing of the President's bell or the shouted 'Chut! Chut!' of the ushers appealing for silence.

The speakers who followed were no more interesting, and Richard began to examine the people sitting with him in the gallery. They were a strange mixture, varying from well-dressed and very respectable men, or foreigners perhaps on business in Paris, to obvious tradesmen of the city, and unshaven and unwashed men and women whose faces appalled Richard. Never had he seen such naked ferocity before; here at last he was looking at some of the Paris mob who had fired the Bastille, stormed the Tuileries and massacred the prisoners last September, and who had horrified all Europe with their savagery. They were following the speeches closely, and occasionally applauding with frenzied shouts.

Richard was turning back to watch a new speaker who had just walked across to the pulpit when he noticed someone looking at him from the back of the gallery. He did not see the face for more than a second, except to notice a blue coat and a turn of the light-coloured hair. Richard frowned, and pretended to listen to the speech below. But that man, who-ever he was, had been watching him. He half turned his head quickly. But the blue coat had gone. Richard shrugged his shoulders. He was imagin-ing things, of course, he decided. Living in hiding in Paris, as he was, he always felt this uneasiness, that people were looking at him suspiciously.

But as he sat there, his long legs cramped by the narrow benches in front, he still felt that uneasiness. Someone was still watching him. He turned slowly this time. Four or five men were standing by the door that led down to the entrance and the street outside, and one of these men looked swiftly away as Richard's head came round.

Richard wriggled sideways on the hard bench, as if attempting to find a more comfortable position, but he could watch the door now without having to turn completely round. Yes, the man was looking at him, a fellow in a dark coat with long hair falling to his shoulders.

The atmosphere in the chamber was cold and clammy, but Richard felt a wave of prickly heat pass over him, and he stared down at the scene below, his hands clenched. Well, he would not be caught here, he decided. If he could make his way outside, there would be room to use his hands, and his pistols too, for he never came out without them.

He pushed his way past the man next to him, and made for the door. The dark-haired man was still there, leaning forward now to watch what was happening in the debate, but his eyes flickered towards Richard and then away as Richard walked past him. With a sigh Richard clattered down the wooden stairs, but he stopped just before he reached the bot-tom. There was silence for a moment, and then he heard feet tramping down towards him.

Richard jumped the last three steps, rushed through the doorway, and swung to his left. Ahead lay the gardens of the Tuileries, open now to the public, and filled with a maze of flower-beds and tall hedges. He could lose himself in there quickly enough or, if it came to a fight, then he could deal with this fellow in comparative secrecy.

He walked as fast as he could without actually breaking into a run, for that would have attracted attention. There was no one about here, though, and as he dashed through the gates of the gardens, he glanced over his shoulder. Dark-coat was coming after him, but he was alone.

Richard grinned, though there was little real amusement on his face. Well, this fellow was in for a violent surprise, and the prospect of some action after the boring frustrations of the last week appealed to Richard. He had forgotten his sudden panic up there in the gallery, and as he darted to the left and up a narrow path between the hedges, one hand was inside his pocket and pulling back the cocking-piece of a pistol.

He could hear the hurried patter of the feet, and he moved back against the thick hedge and waited.

Dark-coat burst into view, his white face anxious, but he smiled as he saw Richard.

'Monsieur Carey?' he asked.

Richard gaped at him. This was worse than he had thought. They knew his name, then, so this fellow was an agent of the Government. He pulled out his pistol, and the long barrel glinted for a moment in the dull afternoon light.

'No, *monsieur!* No!' the man said, and he held up his hands as he stepped hurriedly away. 'I am a friend. I have been told to bring you to the Baron's.'

'The Baron? Which Baron?' Richard asked suspiciously, without moving his pistol.

'The Baron de Batz, *monsieur.*'

'Who the . . .' Richard broke off. He had heard that name before. De Batz, de Batz. He grinned, with genuine amusement this time. Of course, this was one of old Rupert's acquaintances. Good old Rupert! He must have got in touch with de Batz somehow, and told him to look out for Richard.

'If you will follow me, *monsieur,*' dark-coat said, relief on his face as he saw the heavy pistol disappear once more.

Richard nodded, but as they set off he still kept one hand inside a pocket, his fingers touching the pistol butt. They went through the gardens, across the wide Place de la Révolution, and into the streets beyond, most of them fairly respectable, and lined with shops and cafés, until dark-coat turned down a quiet road and stopped in front of a large house.

'Here, *monsieur*,' he said, and he tapped on the door.

There was no delay, for it swung open immediately, but only far enough for a face to peer out for a second. The head nodded, and Richard found himself inside a spacious hall. The large town house of some nobleman once, he decided; there was still a magnificent chandelier hanging over his head. Government office now, was the next thought that ran through his head. He had been trapped, after all.

But this was no Government office. He knew that as soon as his feet touched the thick stair carpet, and his eyes fell on the long mirrors hanging on the walls; the air of luxury and even magnificence that was his first impression of the place confirmed this feeling.

His guide was climbing the curving staircase, and Richard followed obediently. A footman bowed on the landing above, and waved a hand to the left, along a wide corridor, with more mirrors, much gilt work and an even thicker carpet. Richard's nose wrinkled in perplexity. There was something oddly familiar about the atmosphere of this place. The house was just a trifle too ornate for a French nobleman's residence; or was he judging that by his knowledge of London houses?

But he was given no time to pin down that elusive memory, for a tall, white-painted door, the panels picked out in gold, was flung open, and he was ushered into a long salon, with the inevitable chandeliers, wall mirrors and profusion of gold scroll-work. Even the ceiling was painted, and at his feet stretched another soft carpet, thick and gaily patterned, extremely expensive but a trifle vulgar, so his fastidious sense of taste told him.

'Hullo, Richard!' a familiar voice said, and a hand clapped him on the shoulder.

'Jeffery!' Richard gasped as he stared into his cousin's smiling face.

II

The Baron de Batz

Jeffery beamed at Richard, obviously delighted with his dramatic surprise; an extremely prosperous Jeffery, too, Richard noticed.

'I wonder who I shall meet next in Paris,' Richard laughed. 'First Bellamy, and now you.'

'Bellamy? Do you mean that odd fellow who was up at Clare with you? What's he doing in Paris?'

'Oh, business of some kind,' Richard said hastily, suddenly remembering that Bellamy and Wilson would not be very pleased to hear him gossiping about their activities. But he need not have worried. Jeffery had already lost interest in the subject of the odd Mr Bellamy; as usual he was absorbed in his own affairs.

'Come and meet the Baron,' he said.

Richard followed his cousin. Jeffery, he realized, had not even asked him yet why he was in Paris.

'Ah, so this is Sir Rupert's nephew,' a rich voice said.

Richard bowed. His first impression of the Baron de Batz was one of size, of good clothes, and of white teeth that gleamed between thick, red lips.

'And how is Sir Rupert?' the Baron asked. 'Baptiste! Wine for Monsieur Carey!' He snapped his long, plump fingers, and a silver tray appeared at Richard's elbow.

Richard sipped his wine and inspected the Baron, who was chatting casually about the weather. He was a heavy man, tall and broad, florid, dark-eyed, with black hair and long side-whiskers, a big nose and an equally large chin. His manner was easy and assured, but there was about him a certain force of personality. Richard was not quite certain if he liked that personality, but he had to admit its power.

The other men in the room were standing in a group by one of the windows, talking in low tones. All of them were well dressed, so much so that Richard was acutely conscious of his own shabby clothes, a state of mind he had never experienced before, and one that aroused his natural irritation and arrogance.

'I saw you in the gallery of the Convention,' Jeffery said. 'I couldn't believe my eyes, Richard. What are you doing in Paris, and in those clothes?'

Richard winced, but he explained curtly the position of the Marquis de Vernaye.

The Baron nodded his black head. 'I remember the Marquis,' he said. 'On the last occasion we met we played cards. I won heavily. I cheated, of course.'

'I beg your pardon, Baron!' Richard exclaimed.

The Baron smiled patiently with the air of a kindly father explaining life to his ignorant and inquiring young son. 'The Marquis had ample funds,' he said. 'I had none. So I cheated.' He shrugged his wide shoulders.

Richard blinked, and sipped his wine to hide his sudden confusion and bewilderment.

'You are not planning to rescue the Marquis, I hope, Mr Carey?'

'We were,' Richard said.

'My dear boy,' the Baron said earnestly, and one of his large hands rested on Richard's sleeve. 'You really must lose these youthful illusions. Sir Rupert would never forgive me if I allowed you to blunder around Paris on such a wild business. You can have no conception of the dangers involved. You must leave Paris immediately. Your passport is in order, I take it?'

Richard was nettled. His self-consciousness about his clothes would have made him prickly enough, without this added insult; anyone might think he was an overgrown schoolboy who had run away from home. He explained what had happened on the beach at Graye-sur-Mer.

A gleam of interest flickered in the Baron's dark eyes. 'A French agent in London?' he said. 'His name, Mr Carey?'

'De Marillac.'

A sudden silence fell on the group by the window. The Baron pursed his thick lips.

'You know of him?' Richard asked.

'We do indeed,' the Baron said. 'He is an extremely dangerous man.'

'I have always told you that, Baron,' one of the other men said. 'I was never happy about his joining our Indian Company affair.'

'You are quite right, my dear Dobruska,' the Baron said soothingly, 'but de Marillac has valuable friends in the Government, and he is better with us than against us. Besides, I have no wish to quarrel with him.'

'Who has?' said another man, and they all laughed.

The Baron had turned back to Richard. The good humour, the friendly air of the polite host, had vanished suddenly, and his dark eyes were hard and suspicious.

'I don't understand, Mr Carey,' he said. 'De Marillac is a very capable man. If he saw you on the coast, and then apparently followed you inland to this other hiding-place of yours why is it that you are now wandering around Paris? How did you escape him? He is probably the finest swordsman in Europe.'

Richard had reached the end of his patience; he was angry and resentful. He loathed patronage and condescension, and both aroused the arrogance that was his worst failing.

'De Marillac is dead,' he said shortly.

'Dead! How?' several voices demanded.

'I ran him through with a small sword.'

They all stared at him. The Baron's suspicious glance had changed to one of respect.

'What did you say this young man's name was, Baron?' asked a white-haired and scholarly looking man

'The Honourable Richard Carey, my dear Abbé,' the Baron said. 'His father is the present Earl of Aubigny, and no doubt you are familiar with the reputation of his grandfather.'

'Ah, yes, of course, that would explain it,' the Abbé said, though Richard could hardly believe that he had caught the correct title. What was an Abbé, a dignitary of the Church, doing in this collection of shady characters?

'Well, it doesn't explain anything to me, Abbé,' said Dobruska.

'Lord Aubigny was the most famous duellist of his day,' the Abbé said.

At that moment a servant announced dinner, and the Baron took Richard by the arm. 'You will dine with us?' he asked, though the question was more of a command than a request.

The dining salon was as magnificently and ornately furnished as the rest of the house. The food was startling. Richard had not met such cooking except in a very few London houses, and as he ate he was still trying to pin down that faint spark of memory. This house, with its luxury, the slightly exaggerated atmosphere of wealth, was something that he had met before. As for the men around the table, not even the richness of their clothes could conceal from Richard's critical eye the fact that several of them were new to this kind of life. He whispered to Jeffery, who was sitting by his side.

'What is all this?' he muttered.

'The Baron's headquarters in Paris.' Jeffery grinned. 'I'm his chief staff officer.'

'Headquarters for what?'

'Making money,' Jeffery said simply. 'We use the house as a gambling-salon, too.'

'Of course!' Richard said. That was the memory, the fashionable gaming-house he had visited once in London, the same extravagant furnishings, the same atmosphere of faint vulgarity.

'Our most important business at the moment', Jeffery was saying, 'is the Indian Company. The Baron is floating the shares all over Paris. Most of the chief Government officials have taken them up.'

'What's the object of the Company?'

'To put money into our pockets, of course,' Jeffery said with the same pleasant candour with which the Baron had discussed his cheating at cards. 'What do you take us for, Richard? A charitable organization?'

Richard shook his head as he looked round the table. No one would have made that mistake after watching these hard-faced men.

'And these others?' he asked.

'Well, that's the Abbé d'Espagnac next to the Baron,' Jeffery said. 'Clever old fellow! Trades under the name of his valet in army contracts. He must have snapped up a quarter of a million in the last three months,' he added with a note of envy and respect in his voice.

'An Abbé! Army contracts!'

'Why not? He must live somehow.'

Richard's shoulders lifted in a gesture of helplessness. 'What about the others?'

'There are the two Dobruskas. They're from Austria, and they are doing very well in the corn business. They give good dinners to Government officials, and then wheedle contracts out of them. You see that swarthy man at the end of the table? That's Alonso Guzman; he's Spanish, and runs a gaming-house, and he dabbles in army contracts as well.'

Richard finished his meal in silence, and listened to the conversation of the others. As they strolled back into the salon he watched Jeffery with mounting bitterness. Jeffery was probably the one really close friend he possessed of his own age, for he was an only son, and had been brought up by an indulgent mother in a small and compact little family circle. Whatever Richard's faults might be – and pride and an exaggerated sense of money and position were certainly two of them – his standards were high. He shrank instinctively from dishonesty and fraud, and the atmosphere of this place with its unashamed greed had bewildered him at first. Then he had been contemptuous, and now he was angry, for Jeffery was involved; however much the Careys might condescend to outsiders, they never deserted their own relations.

'I suppose you've done pretty well yourself?' he remarked to Jeffery.

'Very well. Why?'

'Paid your father back yet?'

Jeffery flushed. 'No, I haven't. You don't approve of all this, do you, Richard?'

'I don't!' Richard snapped.

'It's all very well for you!' Jeffery exclaimed hotly. 'You've got to change your moral standards to suit your condition. I can't afford to have any scruples.'

'Moral standards never change,' Richard said impatiently. 'I just don't like your friends, Jeffery. Look at 'em! Shady financiers, unfrocked priests, gaming-house proprietors from the stews of Madrid, and . . .'

'Who gave you the right to preach to me?' Jeffery demanded. 'I suppose you think you can talk like this because you lent me money. Well, if that's what's worrying you, I'll pay you back now.'

'High time, too.'

Jeffery raised a clenched fist, but Richard caught his arm. 'That's just what you need,' he said. 'A punch on the nose. And don't waste your breath calling me out. I've had enough of duelling.'

'You can say that easily enough,' Jeffery said bitterly. 'No one in Europe in his right senses would call you out now that you've killed de Marillac.'

A rich, soothing voice broke in on their squabble. 'Now, what is all this?' the Baron asked. His dark eyes flickered from one angry face to the other.

'Richard doesn't approve of us, Baron.'

'Naturally not,' the Baron said heartily. 'He is an honest young man.' His florid face and thick, red lips creased in a smile of genuine humour.

'Well, he was infernally rude,' Jeffery said.

'So you lost your temper, eh?' The Baron shook his head in reproof. 'That disturbs me, my dear Jeffery. The most engaging feature of your character is your complete lack of scruple over money. That and your air of innocent youth make you a most valuable assistant. But once your conscience begins to trouble you, then you will become quite useless to me. Eh?' The Baron's tone was light, but there was a note of warning in the rich voice.

'Sorry, Richard,' Jeffery mumbled.

'Yes, I lost my temper, too,' Richard said, and he smiled at his cousin, though perhaps only the Baron noticed that he made no apology.

'Well, that is settled,' the Baron said. 'Now we have business to discuss, Mr Carey, and you must excuse me. You must visit us again whenever you wish. We are always open in the evenings for business, and if you wish to play at the tables, consult Jeffery. Some of the tables are run honestly.'

There was a swing and a purpose in Richard's walk as he made his way back to the Rue St Honoré. At last, he thought, there was a chance of breaking through the fog of boredom and frustration that had hung over them since they arrived in Paris, and his brain was beginning to work again.

He found Armand sitting despondently over the fire, and he told him quickly what had happened.

'Do you know anything of this man de Batz?' he asked. 'He calls himself a Baron, too.'

'Oh, that's his correct title,' Armand said. 'Father knew him, I believe. He has a very doubtful reputation, Richard.'

'There's no doubt about it at all,' Richard said. 'He's a capable scoundrel. But he has close connections with the Government, and he could help us.'

Armand swung from gloom to optimism in one of those swift changes of his temperament, but Richard shook his head.

'Don't expect too much,' he said. 'I've a plan, but it's a crazy one. Now, if Duport has finished those clothes for us, we'll visit the Baron tomorrow night.'

Duport had finished the clothes, and the following evening Richard dressed himself with some care and a good deal of satisfaction. The cut of the coat was new to him, but the cloth was excellent, and as he surveyed himself in the long mirror, much of his old self-assurance returned. He had never realized before how much his clothes had added to his confidence, and he would need it all to persuade the Baron to help them.

They were admitted to the Baron's house without any hesitation. Clothes again, Richard decided, as a footman took their coats, and a second man led them up the wide staircase. Armand was looking about him with some animation, much more like the young man Richard had first met at Vernaye.

'Do you know this house, Armand?'

'I do,' and Armand laughed. 'It belongs to old Charles de Pointevin. He was one of the first to emigrate, and all his estates were confiscated. Not that that would worry him; they were all heavily mortgaged. He had to sell most of the pictures and carpets here to pay his gambling debts. I must say the house is smarter than it was in his time.'

There were thirty or so men and women in the main salon, standing by the side-tables laid with food and wine. Double doors at the far end led into another room, and Richard could see the round green-topped tables and the circles of intent faces.

The Baron saw them, and came across the room. His manners, as he greeted Armand, were faultless, as even Richard was forced to admit.

'It is a pleasure to see some of the old families here again,' the Baron said. He surveyed the people in the room with a benevolent contempt. 'Mainly riff-raff, as you see for yourself, Vicomte. Thrown up by the Revolution.'

'You don't turn them away, though,' Richard said. Though he needed the Baron's help, he could not resist prodding him, and if he could attain even the smallest moral advantage, he would have won the first round.

'My dear Mr Carey!' the Baron said. 'We turn no one away. At least, only those who look as if they have no money. If they come here just to drink my wine, or eat a large supper, then they are directed to the tables in the next room. You must pay for your pleasures.'

'Of course,' Richard said. 'But I'm not much of a gamester, Baron. How much must I lose at the tables before I can have my supper? I'm very hungry.'

The Baron chuckled, and he eyed Richard with an amused respect. There were probably few men, if any, in that room who could insult him with such politeness as this.

'My house is yours, Mr Carey,' he said. 'Your uncle, Sir Rupert, once saved me from complete ruin, and I have never been able to repay him.'

Richard's eyes flickered as he heard this, and his confidence grew. But the Baron had noticed his expression, and misunderstood it.

He chuckled again. 'You are quite right, Mr Carey,' he said. 'I seldom tell the truth. I suppose I must be the most accomplished liar in Europe, just as you are the most dangerous swordsman,' and he bowed as if to an equal. 'But I was speaking the truth then. I beg you not to tell Jeffery, though. He would lose all confidence in me.'

Richard bowed and smiled. There were times when he liked the Baron. 'You can repay Rupert,' he said.

'Indeed! How?'

'By helping us to release the Marquis de Vernaye from the Abbaye prison.'

There was silence for a moment as the Baron stroked his black side-whiskers; his eyes were watchful now, for this had become a matter of business.

'That is impossible, Mr Carey.'

'Not for you. I can tell you exactly how to do it. You need not worry about the money. I can provide that.'

The Baron's face twitched. That mention of money was a shrewd thrust from Richard, and it had slid neatly through the Baron's guard. He might be the liar and scoundrel that he openly admitted to being, but he still considered himself a gentleman.

'There will be no need for that,' he said quickly. 'Yes, I would like to hear your plan, Mr Carey. Jeffery will bring you to my private room later in the evening.'

Armand caught Richard's arm as the Baron bowed and stalked away.

'Richard, you sound very certain about this,' he said.

'I'm not. But I want to give the Baron that idea. Look, there's Jeffery over there. You've never met him, have you?'

They gambled casually, drank some of the Baron's excellent wine, and tasted the cold supper. Then Jeffery led them down a corridor at the back of the house, and into a smaller room furnished with a quiet taste that was lacking in the other salons. The Baron was sitting at a desk heaped with papers, but he pushed them away and waved Armand and Richard to chairs.

'Now, Mr Carey,' he said.

Richard drew a long breath. To convince this hard-headed man he must produce a plan with some sense, and state it with a great deal more confidence than he felt at the moment.

'My uncle once told me that the best plan is the simplest one,' he said tentatively. The Baron nodded, still waiting ominously. But now that he had started Richard continued briskly, 'I tried to think of the simplest way in which the Marquis could be moved from the Abbaye.'

'And what would that be, Mr Carey?'

'To go to the prison and ask for him.'

Jeffery snorted with laughter, and Armand's face, so full of hope, dropped in dismay. But the Baron held up one large hand.

'Go on, Mr Carey. You interest me.'

'If an agent of the Committee of Public Safety went to the Abbaye prison and handed the Governor an order from the Ministry of Justice for the removal of the Marquis, then the Governor would hand him over.'

'He would undoubtedly,' the Baron said. 'But first you must find your Government agent.'

'That could be me,' Richard said. 'Or perhaps Armand d'Assailly. His French is better than mine, of course.'

'And the authority to prove his identity?'

'Here,' and Richard threw on to the desk the papers that had come from de Marillac's pockets.

The Baron poked at the papers with his podgy fingers, first almost casually, and then with growing attention. His dark eyes were gleaming as he looked up again at Richard.

'Yes, Mr Carey. And now the order from the Ministry?'

Richard relaxed in his chair. He had won the first two rounds, but the most difficult part of the struggle still lay ahead.

'Who is the Minister of Justice?' he asked.

'Danton.'

'He takes bribes, doesn't he?' Richard said.

'Oh, he does,' the Baron answered. 'I've given him a great deal of money, but he has never done anything for me in return yet.' He stroked his whiskers in genuine bewilderment. 'You see, Danton is also a patriot, besides being a man who does not intend to die poor. So however large the bribe, he will still take it, and then do nothing that might injure France. Most remarkable, isn't it?'

He had asked the question quite seriously, and Richard fought back a smile.

'He must sign a good many papers each day,' Richard said.

'Hundreds. All the ministers are overwhelmed with work.'

'Then he can't possibly read everything put in front of him,' Richard said eagerly. 'From what I know of Government departments, a good many of those papers will be just forms for him to sign.'

The Baron leant his full chin on his hand and stared at Richard. 'Yes, that is so,' he said. 'Go on, Mr Carey.'

'Now, if some clerk in the Ministry is bribed, he could make out a form for the transfer of the Marquis, push it in front of Danton with a pile of similar forms, and there you are.'

'Possibly,' the Baron said. 'Where will you find the clerk?'

'I won't,' Richard said. 'But you can, Baron. Don't tell me that you haven't dozens of them on your list of employees.'

The Baron stared at Richard for a few seconds longer, then he put his big head back and began to laugh.

'Oh, don't you think that would work?' Richard said blankly, for he was sure that he had convinced the Baron.

The Baron's deep chuckles subsided at last. 'I think the whole plan might work extremely well, Mr Carey. Now I know why Sir Rupert had such a high opinion of you.'

'First I knew of it,' Richard said. 'Right, Baron! I thought that if a squad of mounted National Guardsmen accompanied Armand and myself to the Abbaye, then that would add a certain air of . . .'

'National Guardsmen?' the Baron said. 'Now, really . . .'

'These friends of yours in the next room,' Richard said. 'They deal in army contracts, don't they? Uniforms, for instance? We only need a dozen, and I'm sure you can find twelve men who can ride.'

The Baron was startled, and to judge by the expression on his face, he was not often so taken aback. But he recovered quickly.

'When this is over, Mr Carey,' he said earnestly, 'you must join forces with me. In a few months we could have all Paris in our pockets.'

Richard shook his head, and grinned. 'No, thank you, Baron. I'm afraid I should be too honest to be of any use to you.'

'*Touché!*' the Baron said, and he laid a hand on the breast of his blue coat. 'A pity, though. Still, it is refreshing to meet a really honest man occasionally. Very well, Mr Carey. I will find your clerk in the Ministry for you, the uniforms and the twelve men who can ride. That is a master touch, that.'

'And I've got to make certain that the Governor of the Abbaye prison has never met de Marillac,' Richard said. 'I think I know who might tell me that.'

'Oh, and who might that be?' the Baron asked curiously.

Richard shook his head. 'Sorry, Baron, but I can't tell you that,' he said, thinking of Bellamy and Wilson.

'What a remarkable young man you are,' the Baron said. 'Jeffery, ring for Baptiste, and ask him to bring in some wine.'

12

Monsieur Salabet

Richard found his way the next morning to the quiet street in which Bellamy and Wilson were living. They were both in the little room on the ground floor, and greeted him politely, but not with any great effusiveness.

'And how's the Baron de Batz?' Bellamy asked.

Richard gaped at him. 'How did you know I'd been there?'

'Oh, we're interested in the Baron. We saw you and the Vicomte go there last night.'

Richard shrugged his shoulders. He was not particularly curious about the work that these two were doing; even if he was, they would obviously not tell him anything. He told them of his plan to move the Marquis from the Abbaye prison, and they listened carefully, Wilson still and silent, Bellamy nodding his big head and tugging at his fingers.

'I want to know if the Governor of the prison has ever met de Marillac,' he said. 'Do you think you could find that out?'

Bellamy looked at Wilson, and they both nodded. 'We can try,' Bellamy said. 'What are you going to do if you get the Marquis out? Make for the German frontier?'

'I'd rather try the Channel, and find a boat,' Richard said. 'But the Baron can't help us there. Can you?'

Bellamy's fingers cracked loudly. 'I can, as it happens,' he said. 'We send our reports sometimes by fishing-boat from a village on the Channel.' He hesitated. 'I am due in London soon,' he added slowly.

Wilson nodded, and broke his silence for the first time since Richard had arrived.

'Might be safer to have someone with you, Bellamy,' he said. 'I feel nervous about that route. They were confoundedly jumpy the last time I went from there.'

'Yes, I was thinking the same. All right, Mr Carey. You let us know the day you plan to leave Paris. The Baron's the best person to arrange passes for you and the Marquis through the barriers. I've got my own, of course, and I'll meet you at the Baron's.'

Monsieur Henri Salabet paused in front of a large wall mirror, one of many that adorned the gambling-salons of the Baron de Batz, and admired himself for a pleasant minute or so. There was no doubt that his new dark-green coat suited him, he thought. There was an air of quiet distinction about the high cravat and his carefully brushed hair, he decided, as he strutted towards the far end of the room and the table where he usually played.

He took an empty chair, and while the dealer was shuffling the new packs, Monsieur Salabet glanced around at the other players with what he hoped was the correct expression of the hardened gambler, calm, dignified and casual. But no one knew better than himself that he did not possess any of these qualities. He was desperately nervous, and his fingers were shaking as he picked up his cards. Somehow he must win tonight, and win heavily.

He gulped thirstily at the wine by his side; these rooms were always terribly hot, he thought, as he hesitated over his stake, pushed out a pile of counters, hesitated again, and then sat back, his eyes on the dealer.

Standing a few yards away, and facing Monsieur Salabet, was the Baron de Batz. He was watching the little clerk and saw the expression in the man's eyes, and he smiled complacently as he strolled away.

Ten minutes later Monsieur Salabet was finishing his third glass of wine and contemplating with satisfaction the growing pile of yellow counters by his side. His luck was amazing. The cards had not gone so well for several weeks. Another half an hour, and he would have won those vital five thousand francs. He put down his glass with a thump; better not to think about the horrors that might await him if he lost. Somehow, he must repay those francs he had borrowed from the Ministry of Justice.

He lost, and he felt the quick perspiration break out on his forehead. He was a fool to have started this business. But a friend had persuaded him to come one night, and the deference of the Baron, the warm luxury of these rooms, the feeling that he, Henri Salabet, was rising in the new world of the Revolution after so many years of obscurity, had gone to his head. He had won, too, that first night, and he had bought himself that smart green coat, and a new pair of breeches – finer clothes than he had ever worn in his life before.

He had often passed this house in the old days. He had never imagined that he could be a favoured guest here, treated with flattering politeness by a real Baron; titles, of course, were illegal in France, but even a strong republican like Monsieur Salabet had swelled with pride during his first meeting with the affable Baron de Batz.

He staked and lost again; the luck was infernal. He was holding good cards, but the Bank was winning all the time. He grabbed his cards as they slithered across the table towards him. Behind him a quietly dressed man glanced down at the cards, and then over his head to the impassive face of the dealer.

In his private room the Baron was lounging comfortably behind his desk, and chatting to Richard and Armand. Jeffery was turning over a pile of papers and paying little attention to the others.

'You see in me a spider, Vicomte,' the Baron was saying. 'The fly is walking round my web, and then . . .' The big hands spread out for a moment, and then closed. Richard noticed the black hairs on the backs of those capable, powerful fingers, and he frowned. Now that this business had started he was not enjoying it as much as he had thought he would. He felt a sudden pity for anyone foolish enough to walk into the Baron's web; those hands did make him look like a gigantic spider, and Richard had a morbid dislike of spiders. He could not even bear to touch one, though he knew they were harmless enough.

There was a tap on the door, and the quiet man who had been standing behind Monsieur Salabet slipped into the room.

'He has won back three thousand, Baron,' he said. 'Now he is starting to lose. He wants to borrow another three thousand.'

'Let him have the counters,' the Baron said, and he beamed at Richard. 'And more if he needs them. When he has lost them, bring him here.'

The Baron reached for the decanter and poured some wine for Richard and Armand, and then he began to discuss the political situation in Paris. Richard tried to make intelligent conversation, while Armand fidgeted restlessly and Jeffery went on quietly with his work.

Half an hour passed before there came another tap on the door, and Monsieur Salabet was ushered in politely.

'Ah, my dear Salabet!' the Baron said. 'What a pleasure to see you! A glass of wine?'

'Thank you, yes,' Salabet said. He sat down on the other side of the desk, and gulped down the wine.

Richard watched him with distaste; the man was frightened. His face was white and strained, and the expression in his eyes reminded Richard of a puppy about to be whipped; there was the same pleading, scared look, and Richard glanced away quickly. Fright in a man's eyes was not a pleasant sight, he had suddenly discovered.

But the Baron was very much at his ease. He was still lounging, and his red lips were smiling affably at the little man facing him. But his dark eyes were missing nothing as he examined his victim with the calculating and detached view of a surgeon already holding the knife, and ready to make the first cut.

'And what can we do for you, Monsieur Salabet?' he inquired.

The little clerk put down his glass. He had had more to drink than was good for him, Richard thought, and his fingers were trembling so much that the glass nearly fell to the carpet.

'Well . . . I've lost very heavily this evening, Baron,' he said.

The Baron tut-tutted sympathetically. 'We all have these bad runs, my dear fellow,' he said. 'A fresh loan, perhaps? I am sure we could oblige such an important official from the Ministry of Justice.'

If there was any sarcasm in the rich, friendly voice, Salabet did not notice it. He was sitting up, and his shaking hands were adjusting his cravat. Perhaps he was giving a pathetic imitation of what an important official should look like, Richard thought, and he wished he could finish this unpleasant business quickly. No, the Baron was no spider. Spiders killed mercilessly but swiftly. The Baron was a cat playing with his mouse, and he was enjoying the game.

'That is just the trouble, Baron,' Salabet was saying. 'I have already borrowed five thousand in counters tonight.'

'Ah, I see,' the Baron said, and he pursed his red lips. 'We have a rule, as you know, my dear Salabet, that any debts over five thousand must be cleared before a patron is permitted to play again. You have come to pay your debts, then?'

'Well, if you could allow me a few weeks, Baron. I am sure that . . .'

'A few weeks!' The Baron's voice had lost some of its friendliness. The cat's claws were reaching out, Richard thought, and he shifted uneasily in his chair. 'We cannot possibly allow that, Salabet. You know our rules?'

'Yes, of course, Baron. But I have always paid in the past,' Salabet said, his voice rising in his anxiety.

'On the one occasion,' the Baron said. 'Five thousand, I think. Where did that come from, Salabet? The Ministry accounts? You handle those, eh?' The Baron had dropped all pretence of affability now.

Salabet wriggled in his chair and shook his head violently. 'Really, Baron,' he bleated. 'You are . . .'

'A word to the Minister of Justice would soon make the matter quite clear,' the Baron said. 'I shall probably be seeing him . . .'

'No, no, Baron!' Salabet screamed, and he leant across the desk, his face such a mask of utter fear that Richard looked away.

'Now, listen to me, Salabet,' the Baron said curtly. 'One word from me, and you will take a ride to the guillotine. You know that, eh?'

Salabet nodded, his frightened eyes fixed on the Baron, his hands twisting and clenching.

'Then we understand each other,' the Baron said, and he leant back in his chair. 'Bring this to me tomorrow night, signed by Danton, and we will forget your debts.' He handed Salabet a sheet of thick paper.

Salabet took it, and read it hastily. 'To the Governor of the Abbaye prison,' he muttered. 'But I don't understand, Baron,' he said.

'It seems quite clear to me.'

'But Danton will never sign this! He will ask questions, and . . .'

'How many papers does he sign during the day? Does he read them all?'

'Only the important ones, Baron.'

'Well, he won't read this one. If he does, the worse for you, eh?'

Salabet mopped his forehead and stared pathetically at the Baron. His eyes roved round the luxurious little room, over the faces of the others who were watching him, and Richard could read his thoughts so clearly, his dread of the great Danton, the vision of the guillotine, the choice that confronted him, and then the realization that he had no choice if he wanted to save his neck.

'Very well, Baron,' he said. He stood up, and with some attempt at dignity he bowed slightly, and scurried out of the room.

'Miserable little rat,' the Baron growled.

'Fly, Baron,' Richard said.

'Eh? Oh, yes, I am the spider.' The Baron laughed, and refilled his glass.

'I handled that well,' he said complacently. 'You need a certain flair for this business, Mr Carey.'

'You were superb,' Jeffery said, and the Baron beamed at him.

'He was hardly worth my attention,' he said. 'A child could have handled him. Still, I grant you, my dear Jeffery, I was superb.'

Richard shrugged his shoulders. The whole affair had sickened him, but he supposed that he should waste no sympathy on the wretched little clerk.

'Tomorrow night, then,' the Baron said. 'And then you and the Vicomte can go to the Abbaye prison the following morning, Mr Carey. I should waste no time.'

'The National Guardsmen?'

'That has all been arranged. And passes for the Marquis, yourself and the Vicomte.' The Baron smiled at the two young men cheerfully. 'Yes, as neat a little plan as I have ever devised,' he added.

Richard did not argue the point. If the Baron was now convinced that the whole plan was his invention, then let him think so. The main object was to free the Marquis de Vernaye, and that was all that worried Richard. Perhaps he could then return to Wales with an easy conscience, and with the approval of Rupert. He would have given a great deal for his uncle's praise, he decided, as he walked back through the empty streets with Armand, who was chattering excitably about their chances.

13

The Abbaye Prison

They were all waiting again the next evening in the Baron's room, Armand restless and convinced that Salabet would never bring the order from the Ministry, Richard almost as tense but doing his best to conceal his anxieties, and the Baron completely at his ease, and supremely confident.

Jeffery came in, his face alight. 'He's here, Baron,' he said, and then little Salabet trotted into the room. All his fears had vanished, and he beamed at the Baron as if they were old friends, and the unpleasant interview of the previous evening had never taken place.

'Here it is, Baron,' he said, and he laid the paper on the desk. The Baron picked up the document in his thick fingers, and Richard leant over his shoulder. The sheet bore the stamp of the new Republic at the top, with the subtitle of the Ministry of Justice. But it was at the bottom that the Baron and Richard were looking so eagerly. For there was a large, bold signature, an elaborate 'D' with a great backward curl, a few decisive letters, a large 'T', firmly crossed with a broad scratch of the pen, and the two final letters.

'Yes, that's Danton's signature,' the Baron said. 'Did he say anything, Salabet?'

The clerk chuckled proudly. 'What he always says, Baron. "Give it here, you fool! How many more papers to sign?" And he cursed me and the papers I was holding. But you have heard him, Baron. His language is the foulest in Paris!'

'Yes, I've heard him. Who is the Governor of the Abbaye prison?'

'Citizen Villon. Oh, you need have no fear of him, Baron,' Salabet said confidently, and Richard smiled at the change in the man. The relief at the thought that his debts were now settled, and his delight at fooling the great Danton, had intoxicated him. 'Villon will never question that paper. He is a stickler for orders; one of the old school, Baron.'

'He'd better not question it,' the Baron said grimly. 'If anything goes wrong, Salabet, then it won't take Citizen Samson long to strap you down under the knife.'

All the confidence drained from Salabet; his face went white, and once more he was a badly frightened little man.

'Nothing will go wrong, Baron, I assure you,' he said. 'I will say nothing; nothing to anyone. I swear it, Baron.'

'You won't have a chance,' the Baron said. 'You will stay in this house until the Marquis de Vernaye is well on his way to the frontier.'

'But that is impossible, Baron! I must be at my desk at the Ministry in the morning.'

'You are suffering from a sudden fever,' the Baron said. 'Here is paper, pen and ink. I suggest a shaking hand, Salabet. A feverish hand.' He watched Salabet write, and nodded his satisfaction. 'Jeffery, see that this goes to the Ministry in the morning. And show Monsieur Salabet to a room.'

Richard and Armand arrived outside the Baron's imposing house early the following morning. It was a chilly day, with a damp mist hanging over the Seine, not the weather for a business like this, Richard thought, as he stamped his cold feet on the pavement, and inspected the coach that was drawn up by the house. The coachman was a bulky figure in his big coat, and as Richard looked up he nodded his head and grinned.

'Paul!' Richard said. 'I didn't know he was in Paris, Armand.'

'He arrived three days ago. I haven't had much chance to tell you with all the arrangements we've been making.'

They went inside the house to have a last word with the Baron, and found Bellamy there, chatting to the Baron and tugging at his fingers in his usual fashion.

'Ah, there you are,' the Baron said. 'They are bringing the horses round now, Mr Carey. You had better ride to the Abbaye. Baptiste! The two sashes!'

Richard and Armand opened their coats and stood there while the Baron's servant tied the sashes, the badge of the Government agent, around their waists.

'The National Guardsmen will meet you at the Abbaye in thirty minutes,' the Baron said. 'You would look conspicuous with such an escort leaving this house. They will leave you when you are safely away from the Abbaye.'

They rode through the streets with the coach lumbering behind them, and Armand, who knew his Paris well, guided them down the Rue de Sève.

'Nearly there,' he said to Richard.

Richard nodded and tried to fight down the sensation of tenseness that was sweeping over him. He must appear casual and relaxed at the Abbaye, but he knew that that would probably be impossible. At the least, he must try to look the part, even if he felt far otherwise.

He wondered about Armand. His cousin was an excitable young man; his temperament could hardly be described as quiet; was he the man for a cold-blooded piece of work like this?

'Here we are,' Armand said, and he stopped outside a tall building with tiny, barred windows and great double doors that were firmly and grimly closed.

'No sign of those Guardsmen,' Richard muttered.

'Oh, they'll be here, I expect,' Armand said quietly, and Richard glanced at him. Armand was sitting in his saddle as if he were on a casual outing at Vernaye, and his voice was calm and unhurried.

'Anyway, I'm not going to wait,' Armand said as he dismounted.

Richard smiled. He need not have worried about Armand; in fact, as he realized with a slight shock, Armand had already taken charge of the affair.

'Turn the coach, Paul,' Armand said. 'Be ready to move quickly. Ready, Richard? I should say as little as possible. Let me do the talking.'

They handed over their horses to one of the Baron's men who was sitting beside Paul, and then, without any hesitation, Armand strode briskly to the great doors and pulled at the iron bell-rope. A small peep-hole opened and a face peered out at them.

'From the Ministry of Justice,' Armand said curtly. 'Orders for the Governor.'

Bolts screeched and one of the doors swung open. A thin man muffled up to the ears in a long coat blinked at them, and carefully closed the door again.

'Take me to the Governor,' Armand said.

'But, yes, Citizen,' the man said. The mere sight of the red sashes and the sound of Armand's imperious voice were quite enough for him.

The heavy lock turned with a thud, and Richard stiffened as he heard that ominous sound. They had managed to get into the Abbaye prison easily enough, but leaving might be a different matter.

The janitor was shambling across a narrow courtyard flanked by high walls pierced at regular intervals by barred windows, a gloomy and forbidding place on that damp, cold morning, with a grey sky overhead that seemed to press down upon them. They went through a door and down a corridor with a stone floor and dirty white walls; the whole place stank of dampness and cold and misery, and Richard shivered. They marched

through a waiting-room, or so Richard assumed it to be, and into a large office with high desks, where two wizened old men were bent over papers. They glanced indifferently at the new arrivals, and then one of them rang a bell.

A prison official came in, and Armand turned to him impatiently.

'Orders for the Governor,' he said, holding up the paper that Danton had signed. 'From the Ministry of Justice.'

'Yes, Citizen. If you will follow me.'

Down another corridor they strode, their boots clattering loudly on the stone floor, while Richard followed Armand's brisk, confident figure, and wished that he could feel so assured. Did his feet sound so firm, he wondered, and then he grinned, despite his mounting pessimism and fear that in a few minutes they might well be arrested themselves. He had suddenly thought of Rupert. Old Rupert would have enjoyed this caper; he would have been in his element now. The smile and the thought of his uncle did Richard some good, and by the time the prison officer had stood aside respectfully to allow them to pass into the Governor's room, Richard had control of his nerves again.

The office was a barely furnished room with high, whitewashed walls, and tall windows that looked out on to the courtyard and the grey brick of the main prison block. A grey-haired man with a prim and petulant face was looking at them inquiringly.

'From the Ministry of Justice,' Armand said for the third time. 'Order for the *ci-devant* the Marquis de Vernaye. And my authority from the Committee of Public Safety.'

He put the two papers on the desk, and the Governor examined them carefully. A fussy, pernickety man, Richard decided, as he noticed the tidy desk, the chairs arranged as if on parade, the neat dress of the Governor himself, and his precise examination of the documents.

'These appear to be in order, Citizen,' he said.

'Naturally,' Armand said, and he glared at the Governor, his manner that of the important official faced with fussy underlings.

The Governor coughed and dropped his eyes under Armand's angry glance. 'I will send for the prisoner immediately.' He tinkled a hand-bell. 'Will the prisoner need all his clothes, Citizen?'

'None,' Armand said. 'We require him for interrogation only. I shall probably return him tonight, or early tomorrow.'

The Governor nodded, and issued his orders to one of his men. Armand sat down as if he owned the entire office, and Richard watched him with admiration. This was going to be easy; there had been no need for any worry at all.

'You know the prisoner, Citizen?' the Governor was asking idly, more for the sake of conversation while they were waiting than for any other reason.

'We met in the old days,' Armand said. 'I have an old score to repay,' he added bitterly, and Richard sighed.

For one of their fears had been the Marquis when he saw Armand. His face might well give the whole game away, but any surprise he showed could now be explained quite simply.

'Yes, quite so,' the Governor said, glancing down at Armand's pass. 'Ah, yes, de Marillac, of course. You know my deputy, I believe.'

There was silence for a moment. Richard clenched his hand and looked sharply at Armand.

'Indeed, and who is that?' Armand asked, and Richard relaxed again as he heard the calm indifference in his cousin's voice.

'Lacoste,' the Governor said. 'He worked with you in Lyon last summer.'

'Yes,' and Armand laughed. 'He did, indeed. And how is he?'

'Very well, Citizen. But you would like to meet him, I am sure.' The Governor's hand reached for the bell. 'I will let him know that you are here.'

Richard opened his mouth, his eyes on the Governor's thin hand as it held the bell. But he could say nothing. What was there to say?

'Please, Citizen!' Armand held up his hand, and the bell was laid down. 'I have no wish to renew my acquaintance with Lacoste. We had a difference of opinion in Lyon. He would certainly not wish to see me, either, I assure you.'

'Indeed,' the Governor said. He was puzzled, but his hand had left the bell, and Richard discovered that he had been holding his breath. 'I am sorry to hear that, Citizen. Lacoste has a hasty temper, I know, but . . .'

Steps were clattering in the corridor outside, and Armand jumped to his feet. He shot a quick glance at Richard, but his expression had not changed. He turned away as the door opened, and a man was pushed unceremoniously into the office.

'The prisoner Vernaye,' the warder said.

Richard turned slowly to look at the Marquis. He saw a tall, spare man, white-haired and haggard with worry. His face was lined and kindly, but dull and lifeless, as if the spirit had been drained away, and he stood there quietly, submissive and helpless.

He saw Richard looking at him curiously, and a faint gleam came into his tired eyes, a gleam of puzzlement, with a slight crinkling of the high forehead. Then he turned to Armand. His mouth opened, and an expression of the most incredulous astonishment passed over his face.

'I see you remember me, Citizen Vernaye,' Armand said harshly. 'My name is de Marillac. We met last at Rouen, I believe.'

'De Marillac?' The Marquis stared at his son, his whole body twitching, and Richard saw the anguish in Armand's eyes. 'Yes, of course, I remember you very well,' the Marquis faltered, and there was a smile in the faded eyes. 'Very well indeed.'

'Here are the prisoner's papers,' the Governor said. He had seen nothing of all this, but had been extracting papers from a folder on his desk. 'If you would sign here, and there? Thank you, Citizen. You have a carriage of some kind?'

Armand scrawled a signature in two places. 'Thank you, I have,' he said. 'If you will excuse us, Citizen? My orders are urgent.'

'Of course, of course,' the Governor said, but Armand was already walking towards the door, and Richard took the Marquis by the arm and gave him a gentle push.

They clattered down the corridors, with the warder leading. The Marquis looked pathetically at Richard, who smiled and winked. But he was far from happy. Armand was walking at a snail's pace, he thought. They ought to be running, not strolling. Then they were crossing the yard, and Richard heard the Marquis draw a deep breath. The janitor came shuffling out of his room by the gate.

'Yes, Citizen?' he said.

'Open the gate, you dolt!' Armand snapped. 'Do you want to keep me waiting all the morning in this cold?'

'No, Citizen, no!' the janitor quavered, looking respectfully at the red sashes. 'But I must make sure that it is in order for you to leave. The Governor's orders, Citizen, you see.'

'It's all right,' the warder said. 'Open up, Jacques.'

They stood there while the man fumbled with his key, the longest few seconds that Richard had ever known. Then the lock clanged back, the door swung open, and there was the coach, and behind it an imposing array of mounted men. Nothing could have looked more official, and Richard felt the Marquis recoil. But he pushed his uncle forward after Armand's trim figure, down the steps and towards the coach.

'Armand!' the Marquis whispered.

'Inside, Father!' Armand hissed. 'No time now! Quick!'

He pushed his father inside the coach, and Richard turned to mount his horse. Then from the gates of the prison came a loud shout.

Richard gulped. The sheer pain of that sudden panic made him gasp as he swung round. A tall man was running towards them.

'De Marillac! De Marillac!' the man was calling. 'What is this tale that old Villon has been telling me? The old dotard's got it wrong, as usual!'

'The Citizen de Marillac is inside the coach,' Richard said. He could speak, he was surprised to discover, and his hand was already pulling out a pistol. He rammed it into the man's ribs. 'Get inside the coach!' he said.

Lacoste stared down at the pistol and then up into Richard's face. But that was as much as he did see. Richard had stepped back; he switched the pistol to his left hand, and his right came up with a thudding upper-cut that caught Lacoste full on his blue jowl. He sprawled backwards inside the coach, and collapsed across the seat.

Armand had leapt down from his horse, and was thrusting a pistol into his father's hand.

'Watch him!' he muttered, and he slammed the door. 'Paul! Drive on! Quick, man, quick!'

Paul cracked his whip. The coach moved forward, and behind came the clattering escort of guards. Richard turned his head. The turnkey was looking out from the gate, but he did not seem to be showing any signs of alarm. Possibly he had seen nothing of the swift incident by the coach. Anyway, it did not matter if he had; it was too late now; they had a few minutes' start, and by the time that precise old Governor had organized a pursuit, or an inquiry – and an inquiry would be the first plan to enter his methodical mind – the coach would have disappeared in the maze of Paris streets, and the bogus Guardsmen would have vanished like ghosts.

14

Escape

Fifteen minutes later the coach pulled up with a jerk outside the Baron's house. The Guardsmen had already turned off, and would be out of their uniform and out of the sight of Paris before anyone could question them. Paul Legendre swung down nimbly from the high seat, wrenched open the door and dragged Lacoste out like a sack of flour.

Lacoste had recovered consciousness by this time. He struggled to his feet, and then Paul's ponderous fist came down on the side of his head like a hammer. With one heave he hoisted the unfortunate man up on to his broad shoulders and rushed up the steps and inside the house.

Armand dragged his father out, shouted to the Baron's servant to drive away the coach, and in a matter of a few minutes the street was empty once more.

The Baron was waiting for them in his small salon. He hastily poured out a glass of wine for the Marquis, who had dropped into a chair and was shaking nervously, his dazed eyes looking round the room like a man who has just awakened from a nightmare.

'It is indeed you, Armand,' he said. 'I could not believe it! And your mother and Louise? Where are they?'

'In Wales, Father. Thanks to Richard here.'

'Richard?' The Marquis stared at Richard. 'Your face is strangely familiar, *monsieur*. I was sure that I had seen you before, but I . . .'

'I'm Richard Carey, Uncle Quentin.'

The Marquis shook his head helplessly and smiled. 'Of course! You are very like your father. Well, well!' He raised a trembling hand. 'You must forgive me, Richard, but this is overwhelming. One moment in the Abbaye prison, and then . . .' He laughed shakily.

The Baron was watching him, and rubbing his hands with delight. The whole plan was his now, Richard thought, and he grinned. There was a somewhat engaging side to the Baron, after all, despite his faults.

'It is a great pleasure to meet you again, my dear Marquis,' the Baron said.

The Marquis looked up. 'De Batz!' he said.

'Yes, Marquis. Your son and nephew came to me for help.' He bowed. 'It was a risky plan, but a challenge to my powers. And I do not often fail, you see.'

'We shall if we don't leave Paris within the next hour,' Richard said. 'What about that fellow Lacoste?'

The Baron raised a large and reassuring hand. 'I shall take good care of him, Mr Carey,' he said. 'Your horses are ready, and your passes to leave Paris. You will leave by the *barrière* at the end of the Rue St Honoré.'

'And after that?' the Marquis asked. 'Which frontier do we cross?'

The Baron shrugged his shoulders almost sulkily. 'That is out of my hands,' he said. 'Your nephew has friends who have arranged for a boat across the Channel.' To judge by the tone of his voice he was annoyed to think that any part of the plan was the responsibility of somebody else; nor did he appear to have any confidence in arrangements made elsewhere.

They were interrupted by the arrival of Bellamy. He bowed hastily to everyone in the room, stammered with some of his old nervousness and tugged fussily at his fingers. But his eyes were darting round the room, and Richard could well believe that little escaped his notice. He had learnt to respect Bellamy's intelligence.

As they rode up to the *barrière*, Richard braced himself for a few unpleasant moments. To his relief there was no special guard there, for if Villon at the Abbaye had raised the alarm, then every *barrière* out of Paris would have been doubly guarded by this time. But there was only the usual handful of scruffy National Guardsmen, the normal group of farm carts waiting on each side of the pole that barred the road, and their papers were taken without any special comment by one of the guards.

Richard sat on his horse and waited patiently. Waiting was by far the worst part of any plan but familiarity did not bring with it any lessening of his fears. He tried to watch the people in the carts and listen to their conversation, anything to distract his thoughts, and then the pole swung up, and Armand was stuffing their papers into the pocket of his riding-coat.

'*En avant!*' he said quietly, and they rode through the gates and out into the countryside beyond.

They reached the coast on the evening of the third day – desperately slow going, but the Marquis could travel no faster. He was a fine horseman, but several months in the Abbaye prison were no preparation for a long ride in the winter, and he was a tired and sick man as they rode down the hill into the fishing village of Crozart.

Richard looked eagerly for a sight of the sea. But what he saw was not inviting or comforting. A strong wind was blowing, and the Channel was a mass of angry grey water with white spray flying over the short quay. Not the weather for taking out a small fishing-boat, Richard realized, and he frowned uneasily. Every additional hour they were forced to spend in Crozart was a danger; and this gale might last for days.

'Too late to find Rigaud tonight,' Bellamy said.

'Rigaud?'

'He's the fisherman we use. There's an inn of sorts here – it's better than nothing.'

Bellamy was right, but barely so, Richard thought as he saw the inn. The rooms were small and dirty, the beds hard, the food atrocious. But the innkeeper asked no awkward questions, though he must have had his suspicions about these horsemen who had arrived so suddenly. But he was well paid with assignats, more than he would normally have earned in two weeks or more, and he seemed satisfied with that.

They sat in the small coffee-room that night, and Richard listened gloomily to the wind as it howled over the inn; heavy rain was pattering on the windows, and he could hear the dull roar of the sea.

'Can you trust this fisherman of yours?' he asked Bellamy,

Bellamy's fingers were cracking nervously. 'No, I can't!' he said. 'But he's been all right in the past. If you offer him enough money, and some gold, I don't think he'll give any trouble.'

Richard grunted uneasily. 'Will he take us right across?'

'There'll be a frigate or a sloop in mid-Channel,' Bellamy said confidently.

'In this weather?'

'Oh, yes, you needn't worry about that, Mr Carey. That's the least of our worries. I sent word to London, and they'll have a boat out there.'

'If necessary I'll take one of these fishing-boats out myself,' Richard said. 'I know enough for that.'

'In this weather?' Bellamy asked, and his fingers cracked loudly.

To add to his comment a particularly violent squall of wind whistled over the village, and the rain dashed against the window as if someone was emptying a bucket of water outside.

Richard shook his head despondently, and they went off to their uncomfortable beds.

The innkeeper produced some bad coffee for them the next morning, with stale, hard bread and rancid butter. Richard poked at his food, and listened to the wind. The weather had hardly changed at all, and from the window he could see the white-crested waves as they rolled into the bay. No fishing-boat could put out in that sea. That meant another day in this dreadful inn. He shuddered. He felt grimy and unshaven; he longed for a change of clothes, but they had brought little with them in the way of baggage. Two days perhaps before he could have a hot bath and a clean shirt and a good shave. He tried to comfort himself by thinking of the inn they would find on the other side of the Channel, the red-faced landlord with his shining, clean-shaven cheeks, the roaring fires, the smell of ham and fried eggs. Richard sighed, and munched miserably at the stale bread.

'Let's go and find Rigaud,' Bellamy said. 'You won't be very impressed with him, Mr Carey. So don't expect too much.'

The fisherman lived in a small cottage near the quay, and they found the man himself in the single room on the ground floor, a filthy place that smelt of fish, bad cooking and damp clothes. Richard's nose crinkled in disgust.

The sight of Rigaud was even worse. He was a big man, surly and indifferent, as if he knew that he had the advantage of them. He shrugged his shoulders when Bellamy told him that they needed his boat.

'Not in this weather,' he said, and he spat on the floor.

'Tomorrow, then?'

Rigaud shrugged his broad shoulders once more, and Richard felt his temper rising. Bellamy's quiet manner would get them nowhere with this fellow, he decided.

'How much?' he demanded.

Rigaud stared at him insolently. 'It's too dangerous,' he said.

'Nonsense!' Bellamy said. 'You've done it before.'

'Times have changed, *monsieur*.'

There was silence for a moment. 'How much is your boat worth?' Richard asked. He had brought out the bag of sovereigns, and was resting it on his knee. The heavy coins clinked with that distinctive sound that any man could recognize, and into the fisherman's eyes there had crept a gleam of eagerness.

'How much?' Richard repeated, and he moved the bag slightly.

'Ten thousand francs, *monsieur*.'

'Nonsense! No fishing-boat's worth that!'

'My life is, *monsieur*.'

'Five thousand, and three good horses,' Richard said, for their horses would have to be left in Crozart.

'Ten, *monsieur*.'

Richard pushed the bag into his pocket and stood up. 'You're wasting our time,' he said. 'There are plenty of other boats in the harbour.'

Rigaud had watched the disappearance of the bag of gold with sullen, calculating eyes. 'Seven and the horses,' he said.

'Six and the horses.'

Rigaud hesitated, spat again and then nodded.

'Show us this boat of yours,' Richard said curtly. He had gained the upper hand, he hoped, and he must continue to do so.

Rigaud led them along the quay and pointed to a boat that was heaving and rolling steadily in the swell. Richard frowned when he saw the boat. She was far too large for one man to sail.

'Well, *monsieur!*' Rigaud said. His eyes were gleaming with malicious amusement. 'Can you sail that boat across the Channel?'

'No,' Richard said.

Rigaud spat violently. 'I will come with you,' he said, 'and bring my boat back. For five thousand and the horses.'

'When can we sail?'

'Tomorrow, *monsieur*. This gale will blow itself out tonight. The tide will be full at noon, and I shall be ready for you, then. You can rely on me, *monsieur*.'

'That's the last thing I should do,' Richard said. 'But you can rely on this,' and he pulled out one of the long-barrelled pistols. Rigaud shrank back. 'If you don't keep your word, I'll blow your brains out,' and Richard turned on his heels and marched away.

'I shall have to find someone else next time,' Bellamy said as they walked back to the miserable little inn.

'Next time!' Richard said. 'Haven't you had enough of this business?'

'I haven't finished my job yet,' Bellamy said calmly.

Richard looked at him with a considerable amount of admiration. 'Well, you're a better man than I am, Bellamy. Once I'm out of France, I shall stay out. I saw the tumbrils on the way to the Place de la Révolution one afternoon. That was enough for me.'

'You get used to that, Mr Carey.'

Richard smiled. 'Do you?' he said drily. 'Well, don't take too many risks, Bellamy. Who's going to look after the family affairs after your father retires?'

Bellamy looked at Richard with some of his old shyness and tugged at his fingers. 'I was hoping to do that, Mr Carey.' His finger-joints cracked loudly. 'If you consider that I should be a suitable person.'

Richard took his arm as they climbed the steps towards the inn. 'I can't think of anyone I should like better,' he said. 'Hullo, someone's in a hurry.'

They paused at the top of the stairs as they heard a horse clattering down the street, and then the rider appeared around the corner of the narrow street, the only street the village boasted. The rider saw them and waved his hand.

'Richard!' a familiar voice shouted.

'It's Jeffery,' Richard said. 'What's the matter, Jeffery?'

'Everything,' Jeffery said. 'Lacoste got away from the Baron's house.'

They all stared at him in horror. Jeffery was obviously exhausted; his boots were covered in mud, his coat and breeches sodden with rain, and as he dismounted he staggered and might have fallen if Richard had not caught his arm.

'Come inside the inn,' Richard said.

Jeffery stumbled stiffly into the coffee-room, and stretched out his legs with a grunt. 'One of the footmen let Lacoste out,' he said. 'Afraid of the guillotine, I suppose, and after a fat reward. Fortunately we heard about it immediately. Too late to stop Lacoste, but we caught the footman. We had time to clear out of the house ourselves. The Baron had a bolt-hole ready, of course.'

'You surprise me,' Richard said sardonically.

'Oh, the Committee of Public Safety would have to get up pretty early in the morning to catch the Baron,' Jeffery said. 'He's safe outside Paris by this time.'

'What about yourself?' Richard asked, looking curiously at Jeffery, and with much the same feeling that Rupert had shown when talking to him on that beach a few months ago.

'Well, I had to come and warn you,' Jeffery said. 'Lacoste knew you were making for the Channel coast.'

'How did he know?' Bellamy asked sharply.

'That footman overheard you talking to the Baron,' Jeffery said, and Bellamy grunted angrily.

'I thought I'd learnt how to keep my mouth shut,' he said.

'Well, you didn't mention the name of the village,' Jeffery said. 'We're certain of that. The Baron questioned the fellow,' and he frowned, as if his memory of that part of the story was not a pleasant one. 'So we've got a start over Lacoste. He's bound to pick up your trail, I suppose. The inns where you changed horses will tell him.'

They looked at each other in dismay, and then their heads turned with one accord towards the sea, their only line of retreat now, and the way home to safety. But there was no comfort for them there in the angry waves that were rolling in steadily and remorselessly from the Channel.

'We must leave here,' Armand said.

'Where can we go?' Richard asked. 'Any more bolt-holes up your sleeve, Bellamy?'

'Not now. There was one other, but it was getting too risky.'

'We shall have to stay here, then,' Richard said. He was not conscious of taking the lead, but the others seemed to defer to him naturally. 'Lacoste may take a couple of days at least to find us. And that fisherman said the weather would clear in the morning. If it doesn't, we shall have to ride for the nearest frontier.'

Bellamy's fingers cracked in his agitation, and he laughed bitterly. 'That will be a long ride, Mr Carey,' he said.

'It's not far to the Belgian frontier,' Richard protested, and then frowned. 'Of course, I forgot. The French have overrun the Netherlands. That means the German frontier, then.'

The rest of the day passed with a dreadful slowness that reduced them all to a despairing gloom. Every footstep in the street brought them to their feet, with anxious faces pressed against the grimy windows. The wind howled dismally over the inn, and the rain pattered on the glass, sometimes with a steady persistence, and occasionally with fierce gusts of lashing fury that showed the wind was still rising. Perhaps the last of the gale, Richard thought optimistically. But it might mean that a fresh gale was blowing up the Channel.

When the light failed they felt a little happier. Lacoste would hardly blunder around the countryside in the dark, and they must be safe now until the morning at least. But they took it in turns to sit up through the night, except for the Marquis, who was still completely exhausted.

When Richard awoke he went straight to the little window of his room. The grey sky seemed to be breaking up at last, he thought, and there were small traces of blue out to sea. The wind had dropped, too, and though there was still a heavy swell, any well-found fishing-boat should be able to put to sea now.

Breakfast, despite the bad food, was the most cheerful meal they had eaten in the place, and even the Marquis had recovered sufficiently to join in the conversation.

'Pack everything, Armand,' Richard said briskly. 'Jeffery, you and Bellamy keep an eye on the street. I'll go down and see Rigaud.' He had assumed the leadership quite naturally, and without even considering the matter, and the others had offered no objection.

Armand cleared his throat and looked at his father with what was almost a sheepish expression. Richard could read his cousin's face so easily now that he wondered what was coming; the Marquis knew his son too, and he smiled.

'You have been trying to tell me something for two days, Armand,' he said. 'What is it?'

Armand gulped. 'I'm not coming to England with you, Father,' he said defiantly.

The Marquis had been as rigidly schooled as his wife in the display of emotion, but his grey brows rose quickly.

'What are you going to do, then?'

'I want to enlist in the armies of France, Father.'

Richard smiled at the dramatic phrase; it was not as he would have put it, but it was Armand's way. The Marquis fumbled for his snuff-box, shook his head sadly when he discovered it was empty, and smiled sympathetically at Armand.

'You don't mind, Father?' Armand said.

'I suppose not, Armand. I don't know. You see, I belong to the France of the past, and there is little here for me now.' He sighed wearily. 'But there may be something for you. So I will not stop you.'

Richard cocked his head to Jeffery and Bellamy, and they went out of the room.

'Well, that leaves four of us,' he said. 'Enough to keep an eye on Rigaud. I don't trust him . . .'

'You'll have to count me out, Richard,' Jeffery said. 'I'm not coming either.'

Richard sighed and leant against the outer doorpost of the inn. 'Don't tell me that you're going to enlist,' he said.

'Not me! I must get back to the Baron.'

'But his game's over,' Richard protested.

Jeffery laughed. 'He's plenty more left to play.'

'I bet he has,' and Richard grinned. 'But I still wish you were coming home, Jeffery.'

'What for? What can I do in England? Father would probably suggest the East India Company again.'

'Well, it did cross my mind that that would be a more honourable service than working with the Baron,' Richard said mildly, and he held up a warning hand. 'Now, don't lose your temper with me again!'

'Not this time, Richard,' and Jeffery smiled with all his disarming charm. 'I think I must be fundamentally dishonest, you know. I like the Baron, and you must admit that life with him is interesting.'

'It's certainly that,' Richard said drily. 'Have it your own way, Jeffery. When you want a change, don't forget me. As Armand would put it, my purse and the family interests will always be at your service.'

They laughed and exchanged mock bows that concealed a great deal more affection for each other than either was prepared to admit. Richard inspected his pistol and then pushed it back into the pocket of his coat.

'That's a frightening-looking weapon,' Jeffery said. 'Not expecting trouble with Rigaud, are you?'

'Not particularly. But I've become so used to walking about with a loaded pistol in my pocket that it's become second nature to check the priming every now and then. This is one of Rupert's pistols. He would be delighted if he saw me now, I expect.'

'He'd have a belt stuffed with them,' Jeffery said.

Richard raised his hand, and strolled down the street. There was no one about, and in any case the entire village consisted of only a handful of cottages. The sky was clearing quickly now. There was a steady breeze – just what was needed to blow them safely across the Channel. Richard began to whistle softly. In twelve hours he would be sitting in a comfortable English inn, with a well-cooked meal in front of him, a deferential waiter at his elbow, and a coach and a team of good horses waiting outside to whisk them down to Wales and the comfort and peace of Llanstephan.

Rigaud was standing outside his cottage. To judge by his appearance, he had neither washed nor shaved since Richard had spoken to him last. He nodded sullenly to Richard, and spat loudly.

'When will you be ready to sail?' Richard demanded.

'In two hours. The horses, *monsieur?* Where are they? You promised me the horses.'

'They're at the inn. I've told the innkeeper that they are yours.'

'And the money?'

'You can have half now, and the rest when we land in England or board a British warship.' Richard produced a wad of assignats and watched while the fisherman counted them slowly and carefully. Then he stuffed them into a pocket and spat his satisfaction.

'In two hours, *monsieur*,' he said.

Richard nodded and strolled back to the inn at the same casual pace, still whistling happily. This crazy business was over at last. A few months at Llanstephan would be bliss after the hunted and uncomfortable life of the last few months. It would be pleasant to show Louise the countryside around his home. Did she ride, he wondered. He might as well go round by the stables of the inn and give orders about their horses, he decided, as the thought of riding entered his head.

He halted abruptly. In the yard behind the inn were four strange horses. They had been ridden hard, to judge by their appearance, and the single ostler that the inn boasted was unsaddling them.

'Whose horses are those, Jacques?' Richard asked quietly.

The ostler had not heard Richard enter the yard, and he jumped round with a frightened look on his face. He eyed Richard uneasily, and then glanced at the back door of the inn furtively.

'One man from Paris, *monsieur*,' he said. 'The others are National Guards from Becque.'

Richard stiffened, and the hand that was still in his pocket closed around the butt of his pistol. His happy dreams had vanished. Lacoste was the man from Paris, and he must have picked up an escort at Becque, which was the nearest town to the coast. And somehow, presumably, they had entered the inn without being seen by Bellamy or Armand.

'Put those horses in the stables, and stay there,' Richard said to the ostler. He pushed a bundle of assignats into the man's hand.

The ostler looked down at the money. His anxious eyes watched Richard, and it was easy to read his thoughts, his greed for the money balanced against his dread of the men from Becque. But Richard gave him no time to make up his mind. All he wanted was time to enter the inn without the alarm being given. Though what he could do when he got inside, he could not imagine.

He opened the back door and found himself in the kitchen, a grease-ridden and filthy place, but there was no one there. He walked across the stone floor and gently pulled the door towards him until he could peep into the hall beyond.

The hall was empty too, but he could hear voices from the coffee-room. They must all be in there, Lacoste and his three men, and the Marquis and Armand and Jeffery and Bellamy. Lacoste had made one mistake. He had not left a guard outside the door.

Richard pulled out the screw-barrel pistol. The second one was in his room with his baggage. But he was wearing his sword, and in the confined space of the hall and the coffee-room a sword in the hands of a man who knew how to use it might be more effective than a pistol.

He put the pistol in his left hand, and drew his sword. He could fire with the left hand if necessary; accuracy of aim would not matter much at point-blank range. Then he stepped into the hall, and crept towards the door of the coffee-room.

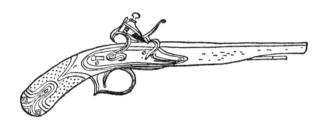

15

The Channel

He stopped by the door and put his head close to the thin panel. He could hear the buzz of voices, but it was impossible to distinguish any words. Now that he had reached this point he still had no idea of his next move, but then he realized suddenly what he would have to do, if he wanted to save his own life and those of his friends inside.

He must shoot the first man he saw with the one bullet he could fire; he would have to run the others through the body without the slightest hesitation or compunction, whether they were unarmed or prepared to defend themselves. In a few seconds he must murder four men, if he could.

Richard's fingers twitched on the grip of his sword, and he drew a deep breath. He could not possibly do this, he decided. Then he heard steps tramping towards the door, and he leapt back against the wall, knees bent, the heavy pistol at the aim, his knees bent ready to lunge with his sword.

The door swung open, and a man stood there in the uniform of a National Guardsman, his back to Richard, and his head turned towards the window of the coffee-room. A rasping voice was speaking.

'. . . the other man in the street, perhaps, Gouvion.'

'Yes, Citizen Lacoste.'

Richard set his teeth. One swift lunge through his back would do the trick. He edged forward, but he could not do it. Then the man closed the door, turned and saw Richard. He opened his mouth to shout; the long blade flickered forward, and the wretched man was pinned against the wall. Richard caught him and lowered him gently to the floor. He scowled down at him, bitter, resentful, angry with himself and with this poor fool who had made him commit such swift and efficient murder.

Still, there was a pistol in the fellow's belt, and that might be useful. Richard stuffed it into his pocket and then clumsily, for his hands were occupied with sword and pistol, he slowly turned the knob of the door. He knew his next move: swift, violent action. Overwhelming surprise would be his best plan, the simplest, too. There was no time for complicated moves now.

He stepped back, brought up his heavy riding-boot and kicked the door open with one smashing heave of his foot, and leapt inside the room.

By the window was a man in uniform. Richard did not pause. The pistol in his hand exploded with a crash and a gush of smoke, a deafening report in that small, overcrowded room. For a second everyone there stood motionless, staring in utter bewilderment. But Richard was still moving. He dropped the useless pistol, his right foot slid forward in a murderous lunge for another uniform. A pistol went off with a roar and a flash; a window smashed with a tinkle of falling glass, voices shouted and figures stumbled together in a confused jumble of coats and breeches. Only Richard knew what was happening, and even he could not possibly take in the whole scene, so swiftly had everything happened. Then the burly figure of Lacoste cannoned into Richard and leapt into the hall.

Richard wheeled round, tugging out the second pistol he had picked up. He pressed the trigger, the powder flashed in the pan, and Richard hurled it at Lacoste. Misfire, he thought as he jumped through the door in pursuit.

Lying across the floor was the first man he had killed. Richard stumbled over him, lost his balance and sprawled flat on his face, his sword dropping from his hand, the blade tinkling on the stone flags of the hall.

He saw Lacoste turn, and a hand come up with a pistol, the round black muzzle pointing straight at his face. A figure jumped into the hall from the coffee-room, arms outstretched, and in between the pistol and Richard. It was Jeffery, shouting at the top of his voice, possibly in the hope of distracting Lacoste, who fired.

Jeffery staggered back against the wall, one hand to his chest, and Richard groaned with fury as he rose to his feet and went for Lacoste, fists swinging, all compunction gone now, and filled with the frantic urge to batter and destroy. His right caught Lacoste on the side of his head, his left made the man double up. But he was strong – stronger than Richard had expected. He kicked out like a mule, and Richard went back, his face twisted with pain, and Lacoste rushed after him, two hands stretched out for the throat.

Richard sent in two jabs to the body. He heard Lacoste grunt, but those hands were still tight around his throat, and Richard gasped for breath as he butted viciously with his head. Then his throat was free, and he swung at Lacoste with both hands, sending him toppling back against the stairs.

From the coffee-room door came a flash and a report. Lacoste spun round as the bullet hit him, one hand grasping for the banister of the stairs, and then he was lying on his face.

'Couldn't shoot before,' Armand said, stepping forward, pistol in hand. 'You were too close.'

'Jeffery!' Richard exclaimed. 'Lacoste shot him.'

Jeffery was huddled against the wall in an untidy heap, and Richard turned him over gently. Blood was trickling from the corner of his mouth and from a round hole in the front of his coat.

'Through the lungs,' Richard muttered. 'Take his knees, Armand.'

They carried Jeffery into the coffee-room while Bellamy cleared a space by the window, and propped up Jeffery's head. The Marquis knelt down, and shook his head sadly.

'The lungs, Richard,' he said. 'There is nothing any doctor could do, even if we could find one.'

'Yes, I know. It's hopeless,' Richard said bitterly. 'My fault, too. Lacoste was trying to shoot me. Jeffery jumped in front of me.'

The Marquis patted his shoulders. 'It was nobody's fault, my dear Richard,' he said.

'I'll stay with him,' Armand said. 'You and Father and Mr Bellamy must get down to the quay.'

Richard rubbed his face in despair and grief. He could not decide what to do next, and he looked pathetically around at the others. He saw the scared face of the innkeeper looking into the room. There were four dead men to account for, and he would have many explanations to make. Richard half smiled. Well, the fellow could do his own explaining, and the thought made his brain turn to action once more.

He looked down at Jeffery's white face, and shrugged his shoulders as if in farewell, for there was indeed nothing more that he could ever do for Jeffery except wait by his side until he died.

'Come on, Bellamy! And you, Uncle Quentin. We must find Rigaud!'

They hurried down to the quay and found the fisherman standing outside his ramshackle little house. He stared at them and greeted them with his usual gesture of spitting.

'There has been shooting, *monsieur*,' he said.

'Yes. And we want to sail in an hour or less,' Richard said.

Rigaud shook his head. 'I can't take you, *monsieur*.'

Richard had reached the point where fury, desperation and grief had made him a dangerous person to cross. His pistol was unloaded, but there was still his sword, and the mere sight of a naked blade was a far more intimidating sight than the muzzle of a pistol.

He stepped back, whipped out his sword and pushed the point forward until it was touching Rigaud's coat. Rigaud recoiled; his back was against the wall of his cottage, and he could move no farther. He squinted down in horror at the long blade that tapered gracefully to the deadly tip resting so gently against his chest.

'You can't kill me, *monsieur*,' he said. 'Who will sail my boat for you, then?'

'I will,' Richard said. 'We are desperate, Rigaud. You can have your choice. Take us out to sea, or I'll spit you.'

His hand twitched, and the tip of his sword slid through the rough cloth of Rigaud's coat; the fisherman squirmed and writhed as he felt the prick of the blade on his skin. There was a note of utter conviction in Richard's voice, but the look in his eyes alone would have convinced Rigaud.

'I will take you, *monsieur*,' he said.

'Right!' Richard did not move the sword. 'Bellamy, get our bags from the inn. Use your pistol if the landlord is difficult. Armand will give you a hand down with the stuff.'

Bellamy nodded, and hurried away. As Richard moved his sword at last, Rigaud drew a deep breath.

'I will row out to my boat, and bring her to the quay, *monsieur*.'

'Oh, no, you won't!' Richard said sharply. 'We're coming with you.'

Rigaud nodded so reluctantly that Richard knew he would probably take the first chance of turning against them. They went down the steps of the quay with him, and Richard helped the Marquis into a rowing-boat, and then scrambled in clumsily after Rigaud. He was too tall to move easily in these small boats, and he was glad when they boarded Rigaud's smack.

She was as dirty and neglected as he might have expected after seeing Rigaud, with untidy piles of ropes, an unwashed deck and an overpowering stench of fish. Richard's nose wrinkled as he wondered what Ianto Price would have said, and he yearned hopelessly for the sight of the Welsh smuggler with his unshakeable composure, and his well-found boat.

But Rigaud appeared to know his trade. He brought the smack along-side the quay in a matter of minutes, neatly and efficiently, and there waiting for them were Bellamy and Armand with the saddlebags.

'How's Jeffery?' Richard asked.

'Just the same, Richard,' Armand said. 'But it won't be long, you know.'

Richard nodded wearily. He loathed the thought of leaving Jeffery to die in that inn, with only Armand by his side in the squalid coffee-room. But what else could he do?

'What about you, Armand?' he asked.

'Oh, I know where to go, Richard. I shall be in the army in a week.' He put his arms round Richard, who submitted stoically to the French form of farewell and listened with embarrassment to Armand's profuse praises of all that he had done.

'I wonder when we shall meet again,' Armand said.

'Sooner than you think, perhaps.'

'Why, are you going to be a soldier too?' Armand asked.

'I suppose so, if we go to war,' Richard said. 'The Careys usually join the army. Don't leave Jeffery yet, will you, Armand?'

'I will wait until the end.' He ran up the steps to the quay and raised his hand.

Rigaud had already hoisted the single sail, and Richard looked out to sea. There were patches of mist stealing over the water, and that might well be an advantage, he thought.

The Marquis went below, for he was still easily tired, while Bellamy stayed on deck with Richard. Neither of them trusted Rigaud, and they would take it in turns to watch him.

An hour later, with a steady wind behind them, they were well out in the Channel, with the French coast a low, dark line in the distance. Richard had hoped to see the English side by this time, but the visibility was too hazy, and they had already run through several patches of mist. The sea was not rough, but the motion of the smack was too much for Bellamy.

His face had paled quickly, and though he had refused to go below when Richard had first suggested it, he staggered down later to join the Marquis.

Richard was squatting on a pile of rope; his own stomach was none too easy, and the rope made an extremely uncomfortable seat. But he was reasonably content; they had not yet seen a British frigate, but then he had never been very optimistic about that. If this wind held, they should reach the English coast in a few hours, and then . . .

Rigaud pulled the tiller over sharply. The smack heeled, and Richard scrambled to his feet. The Frenchman was staring over his shoulder, and through the mist a large lugger was heading straight for them.

'A patrol-boat, *monsieur!*' Rigaud said. 'I must heave to.'

'Oh no, you won't!' Richard said. He rammed his pistol into Rigaud's side. 'Keep on your course.' He cocked the pistol, and the click made the fisherman stiffen. But he pulled on the tiller obediently.

Richard wedged himself against the low bulwark. He wished he knew more about sailing. That lugger was larger than the fishing-smack, so presumably they were certain to be overhauled; there was about a mile between them now.

The smack rose to a wave and rolled violently. Richard staggered, put out a hand to steady himself, and a heavy fist smashed down on his wrist. The pistol clattered on the deck, and as Rigaud let go the tiller, the heavy boom of the sail swung over and caught Richard in the back. He went down, sprawling untidily on the deck. A boot thudded into his ribs, and he rolled away, gasping with the pain.

He saw the boot coming again, and wrenched his head to one side as he came to his hands and knees. The smack rolled, and Rigaud stumbled, thus giving Richard enough time to stand upright. But the fisherman was accustomed to the small deck and the violent motions of his boat. He flung his long arms around Richard and they crashed against the bulwark.

Richard was bent backwards under the man's weight. Another second and he would be over the side. He jabbed Rigaud in the ribs and tried to force him back. But his arms were pinned down, and he butted viciously

with his head. Rigaud grunted, and then the boat rolled again, and across the deck they both went in a heap.

Richard was up first this time, and he swung with both hands at Rigaud. But the boat was rolling heavily in the swell, and he could barely keep his balance. One fist landed, and Rigaud flung his arms around him again. Once more they staggered across the deck, but this time Richard twisted to one side, and it was the fisherman whose back was against the bulwark as they panted and wrestled desperately. But the Frenchman was too strong for Richard. Rigaud swung him round, and bent him over until he could feel the frightful strain on his spine; just below he could hear the rush of the water waiting for him greedily.

The boat rolled, and over came the boom. Richard saw the thick spar sweeping inexorably towards them, and with a crack it smashed into the back of Rigaud's skull. He gasped and relaxed that dreadful grip on Richard's arms, and then Richard hit him with all his strength, once on the side of his unshaven jaw, and then a right full in the stomach. Rigaud flung up his arms, stumbled back and toppled slowly over the bulwark. Another roll from the smack, as if she was anxious to push her master overboard, and then he was gone, and Richard was reaching for the tiller.

He knew enough to bring her into the wind again; she lurched and pitched with a shower of spray that made Richard duck hastily, and then she leapt obediently forward.

Richard grunted, and glanced over the stern. He saw Rigaud's arms splashing away. The lugger would probably pick him up. But where was the lugger? Richard turned his head, and then he saw her, not more than four hundred yards or so to starboard, heading straight for him. He pulled frantically on the tiller, and the smack dived into a patch of mist.

He wondered what course he was steering now. He had not the slightest idea of direction after that struggle with Rigaud, and this mist was enough to upset a far more skilled sailor than he was. For all he knew, he might well cruise round in circles in the middle of the Channel, though he was not worrying too much about that possibility. The first thing he had to do was to try to shake off that lugger.

He saw Bellamy's white face appear from the hatch, and grinned as he caught the look of astonishment spreading over Bellamy's face when he saw no sign of Rigaud. Richard jerked his head, and Bellamy stumbled over the heaving deck and slumped down beside the tiller. Quickly Richard told him what had happened.

'What about this frigate of yours, Bellamy? Did you have any definite arrangement? Time of meeting, compass point, or whatever it is they use?'

Bellamy shook his head, and gulped miserably. 'Someone told me once that when you're seasick you don't mind if the boat sinks,' he muttered. 'Well, I believe them now.'

Richard grinned again. 'You'll start me off soon,' he said. 'Look, what about this infernal frigate? That coastguard lugger will be on top of us soon.'

'All I know is that a frigate will be off this part of the French coast all the week,' Bellamy said. 'That's how I've been picked up twice so far. But not in a mist like this,' he added gloomily.

Richard grunted, and then they shot out into the sunshine again. He looked round for the lugger. Yes, there she was, and a good five hundred yards farther away, too, heading away from them. But as he watched her he saw the bows swing round, the sail fill once more, and she was on a course that would soon cut them off. Bellamy cried out in alarm, and the fishing-smack heaved and lurched as Richard pulled over the tiller. They vanished once more into the mist, and Bellamy slumped back again to the deck, one hand to his mouth, and his face even whiter than before.

Richard wondered gloomily which way he was heading now. Out into the North Sea, probably. 'We can't go on playing hide and seek like this for long,' he said. 'If the mist . . .'

A dark, blurred shape swept through the mist, a long black hull, and the vague white mass of the sails. It was the lugger. Richard heard the high-pitched shouts, and saw men lining the low bulwark. He wrenched at the tiller, but the lugger came round with them, and shot alongside.

'Shoot, man, shoot!' Richard yelled, and he let go the tiller as he dug into his pocket for a pistol.

Half a dozen men jumped nimbly on to the deck of the smack, and two of them rushed towards the stern, where Richard and Bellamy were waiting for them. Richard raised his pistol, and then hesitated. He had one shot only, and there would be no time to draw his sword.

He dropped his pistol on the deck and shrugged his shoulders in resignation. If Jeffery and Armand had been on board they could have made a fight of it. He stood up and allowed himself to be pushed over the bulwark of the lugger. He saw the frail figure of the Marquis as he was dragged up from below; this was all his fault, he decided. He had made a mess of the whole affair, and he shook his head sadly as he saw the Marquis catch his eye.

'They would have caught us soon in any case, Mr Carey,' Bellamy said. He was tugging furiously at his long fingers. 'Very soon,' he added, reverting in his anxiety to his old trick of repetition. 'Look, the mist is clearing.'

He was right, for the mist was shredding away in wisps over the water, and Richard nodded. That was some consolation, perhaps. Then behind him the Frenchmen broke into shrill cries, and Richard wheeled round to follow their pointing arms.

A three-masted ship had burst into view, a towering black-and-yellow hull broken by the square outlines of gun-ports, a mountain of white canvas, a sharp bow that was flinging up an enormous bow wave, a picture of speed, beauty and menace as she swooped down upon the lugger.

A puff of white smoke shot out from the upper deck, and then came the flat boom of the explosion. A fountain of water leapt up twenty yards ahead of the lugger, and the frigate, for so Richard assumed her to be, came round into the wind and stopped, heaving gently on the swell. Already a boat was being lowered over the side, and as she hit the water, Richard saw the thin oars come out like the legs of a caterpillar.

'Well, your frigate's arrived,' he muttered to Bellamy. His voice shook a little in his sudden relief, a sensation that was almost overpowering, and he saw the Marquis straighten his back, and the blood return to the pallid, strained face.

The Frenchmen stood disconsolately in a group by the stern, stunned by the swift and dramatic appearance of the British frigate. There was not the slightest hope of escape; half a dozen shots from the frigate would shatter their thin hull and bring down their masts and rigging in chaos.

The frigate's long-boat bumped alongside, and a short, tubby figure clambered aboard the lugger. Despite his cutlass and the pistol in his belt he was nothing more than a boy, though he swaggered across the deck with all the assurance of a veteran naval officer.

'Anyone here by the name of Bellamy?' he asked in a high-pitched and somewhat cracked voice.

Richard grinned. Voice just breaking, he thought as he ran amused eyes over the midshipman's white trousers that were strained tightly over his plump legs, and the blue coat that was threatening to burst across his back.

'My name's Bellamy.'

The midshipman's face creased in a smile of relief. 'Oooh! That's a bit of luck, Mr Bellamy,' he said. 'We were just in time. Captain Knowle told me to bring you across and leave the lugger. We're not officially at war, you see, so we can't take her as a prize.'

Bellamy nodded. He gestured towards the Marquis and Richard, and introduced them. 'They are coming to England with me,' he added.

The fat little midshipman rubbed his face doubtfully. 'Captain Knowle didn't say anything about anyone else,' he said. 'Only orders about you, Mr Bellamy.'

The Captain was clearly the supreme being of the midshipman's world. No doubt, Richard thought, he had learnt painfully that the Captain's orders were something that must be obeyed to the smallest detail. But it was too cold to stand on the lugger's deck and argue. Richard pushed the Marquis towards the waiting boat.

'Well, we're coming too,' he said. 'I'll explain to your Captain.'

'Mr Carey's father is the Earl of Aubigny,' Bellamy said hastily as the midshipman still hesitated.

His face cleared. An Earl might perhaps be a more remote being than Captain Knowle, but he was still a possible source of patronage and promotion. And an Earl who was a member of the Government too. Richard could read the boy's thoughts as they dropped cautiously over the side and into the boat.

Richard crouched on his narrow seat, his long legs bent uncomfortably, but he was not complaining. He glanced up at the side of the frigate towering above them, the line of gun-ports, the faces looking down curiously, and he smiled. His job was over at last, and he hoped his father and Rupert were satisfied with him. It would be a long time before he left the comfort and security of England again.

He did not even grumble as he performed the difficult and undignified task of climbing up the side of the frigate, clinging grimly to a rope, and finishing in an untidy heap on the deck above. He stamped his feet with satisfaction on the spotless planks, muttered his thanks to the officer of the watch who had helped him to his feet, and asked for the Captain.

'On the quarterdeck,' the officer said.

Richard nodded. He could see a group of blue-coated officers watching the lugger, and he stalked towards the quarterdeck with all the assurance and certainty of a man who knew what his name and family were worth, and the respect that would meet him when he explained his position. He was as good as back in England now, and there was no need any longer to skulk about like a criminal. Jeffery would have recognized that straight back and the arrogant set of the head as Richard raised his hand perfunctorily and marched up to the Captain of the frigate.

'Captain Knowle?' he said. 'My name is Carey. No doubt you know my father . . .'